Deadheading the Hemlock

Witches of the Poison Garden, Volume 1

JC BLAKE

Published by Redbegga Publishing, 2022.

DEADHEADING THE HEMLOCK

First edition. March 15, 2022.

Written by JC BLAKE.

To my family. May the odds be ever in your favour.

Prologue

"Leofe!" My husband's voice was muffled, his face hidden beneath the pillow. As he bucked beneath me, I contemplated keeping it there.

"Leofe!" There was an edge of anger in his voice.

To be honest, in that moment, I didn't want to stop pressing the pillow down. He had hurt me, and I wanted to hurt him back.

Pinning Gerald down as he shouted my name was not how I'd hoped to spend the eve of my fifty-first birthday. Don't get me wrong, straddling my husband as he lay on our bed was something I'd yearned for, but what had once been a daily burst of energetic, joy-filled conjugal passion, had waned to a weekly, then monthly, and now annual occurrence.

And this wasn't our bed.

And we weren't making love.

Sure, I'd aged over the years, put on a bit of weight, and my libido had certainly taken a dive along with my oestrogen levels, but it was my loving husband who had turned cold towards me. And now I knew exactly why—Cordelia, a dog-grooming blonde with a fat backside, wobbly hips, and cellulite down to her knees.

"Leofe!"

He strained to throw me off. I kept the pillow tight against his face.

"Gerald!" Somewhere behind me I was aware of Cordelia screaming his name. "Get off him! Get out of my house!"

1

Ignoring the screeched demand, I glared at the leopard print pillow pressed against Gerald's face. "How could you do this?" I yelled. "How could you do this to me?"

His response was indecipherable, his efforts at pulling the pillow from his face weaker.

Suffocating beneath me was my husband of thirty years—caught in the act of committing adultery. It had taken a few weeks of sleuthing on my part to find out where he was meeting this new woman, but I'd finally found their 'love nest', a semi-detached house in a quiet cul-de-sac on a newly built estate. It was the pristine kind of house with an immaculate lawn, trimmed hedges, and faux cottage style I despised. Even the road names were a deception—Plum Tree Lane, Apple Blossom Crescent—all set up to make Mr. and Mrs. Perfect believe they'd bought into the dream instead of a cookie-cutter house on a huge estate that had consumed local farmland, eaten into the greenbelt, and destroyed the habitat of countless birds, bats, squirrels, foxes, and deer.

Without recognizing it, I'd realized there was something wrong between us, but it wasn't until Gerald had shouted from the bathroom for toilet roll that I became suspicious and suspected that he was having an affair—again. He'd called for me using her name, not once but twice. On the third attempt he appeared to realise his mistake as the name was cut short and irritated mumblings followed. So, pushing the door ajar just as he'd blustered, 'I'll get it myself then!' I'd thrown the toilet roll into the bathroom knowing full well it would land just out of reach.

I waited for him on the landing then pounced as the door opened, biting back the urge to tell him to wash his hands.

'So, who's Cordelia?' I'd asked, arms folded, ready for a fight though my bottom lip trembled, knowing I was on the precipice of more heartbreak.

'Ey?' He pushed past without making eye contact and headed for the stairs.

'Cordelia,' I'd repeated as he ran down the steps, his creaky knees suddenly no longer painful. 'You called for *me* and used *that* name.'

'Don't be daft,' he'd replied from the hallway and grabbed his coat from the hook.

'You did!'

'Silly cow! Why would I call you Cordelia?' He pulled on his jacket but looked down the short hallway to the kitchen rather than at me, then fumbled in his pocket, keys jangling as he pulled them out.

'Because you did!' I had flung back.

He strode out of sight. 'That's just stupid,' he called from the kitchen. The keys clinked as he unlocked the door. 'You been drinking again?'

Momentarily, I remained silent, his comment a gut-punch. For a few months after my mother passed, I'd struggled with grief and used alcohol to help numb the pain and emptiness her death had hollowed out within me. Gerald had caught me tipsy one afternoon. His contempt had been scathing and I hadn't touched a drop since that day.

'What? No! I-' The kitchen door slammed behind him.

As usual, any effort at confronting him had ended in me being the one in the wrong and now he was accusing me of being drunk! Translated to Gerald-speak that meant I was an 'emotional and neurotic wreck', his words after finding me drunk that afternoon. 'Weird' was a common descriptor when he referred to me, followed by 'silly bitch', and 'stupid mare'. 'Only an idiot would do that, Leofe,' or 'You're a bit weird, you would think that!' My cheeks burned and once again I was left feeling stupid, doubt creeping in.

Had I really heard him call that name?

Had I got it wrong—again?

Gerald was always telling me that I misremembered stuff and got things mixed up, even mentioning 'early onset dementia' when I'd asked him what had happened to yet another item of his clothing I could no longer find, such as the suit that was currently missing. He'd accused me of leaving it at the dry cleaners and said I probably couldn't remember because I was heading for that time in life where women 'got fat, saggy, and became old'. He had friends, he'd said, whose wives were going through the 'change', and they were nightmares too. One of them had even gone 'dry' down there. He'd pointed to his groin and caught my gaze whilst wrinkling his nose as though he'd taken a whiff of something rotten. *Thanks, Gerald!* But now, with the image of Cordelia astride my husband, her cellulite covered thighs and naked bottom seared into my brain, I was proven right. He was the liar! A big, fat, cheating liar! I wasn't going mad or hurtling into post-menopausal decrepitude. I wasn't even menopausal, for heaven's sake, at least I didn't think I was. My mother hadn't hit it until she was well into her fifties so there was life in the old girl yet!

Behind me, chipwood floorboards creaked and, just as I spotted the suit Gerald had accused me of leaving at the dry cleaners hung on the wardrobe door, Cordelia lunged forward.

How long had this been going on?

Pain ripped through my scalp as the woman grasped a hank of my hair and pulled. "Get off him! Get off my husband!" she demanded.

Husband? I froze, the pillow now inches from Gerald's face. "*Your* husband?" I hissed. "Gerald is *my* husband."

"Psycho!" she spat and tugged again at my hair, pulling me to one side.

As I began to topple, with the heavy-set woman's fingers still twisted through my hair, I noticed the photograph on the bedside table. It was of Gerald, and a slimmer version of the lumpy blonde. They looked tanned and happy and were stood on a beach somewhere warm. From the haircut and silk lavender shirt, I guessed it had been taken about five years ago – at least that was when I'd bought him the silk shirt as a birthday gift. In his hand he held a flute of champagne that matched hers. She wore a white wedding dress that made her orange tan seem even darker and her blue eyes pop against fake sunbleached blonde hair.

A wedding dress?

I landed with a thud, one end of the pillow clutched in my hand, the other in Gerald's. He yanked the pillow from my grip and flung it across the room.

"Get out!" Cordelia shouted.

I lay, with the pain of the fall radiating through my hips too stunned to move, my shocked mind paralyzed. Gerald made no effort to help me stand but guilt flitted across his face as our eyes met. Mouth open, he stared, then followed my eyes to the photograph.

"Who is this woman, Gerald? Why did she call *you* her husband? What the hell is going on?"

For a split second our eyes locked then he turned his attention to Cordelia. "She's from work. She's the one I've been telling you about."

"The stalker?"

"Yeah." He blinked several times.

Once again pain seared my scalp as Cordelia curled her fingers around a hank of my hair. Still reeling from Gerald's betrayal, I tottered to the door as she pulled me out of the room.

"You're a psycho," Cordelia hissed. "I'm calling the police."

"Er, no need for that love."

"Are you joking me?" Cordelia fired back, her voice laced with venom. "I want this old cow in the cells. Bloody nutter!"

Fire in my belly ignited as shock turned to rage.

How dare he!

How dare she!

I was being hauled out of the house as though I were a despicable piece of human garbage and Gerald, my husband of thirty years, was doing nothing to stop it.

My skin crawled with humiliation.

Vibrations surged through my core.

I had only experienced this intense sensation once before but had never forgotten it. The hairs on my arms, neck, and scalp prickled and a surge of power emanated from my body so powerful that Cordelia was thrown back into the bedroom.

Electrical charges sparked in the dim hallway.

Enraged, I turned to face them. Gerald was not going to get away with treating me with such disrespect!

As another surge of power grew, Gerald stared at me slack mouthed whilst Cordelia picked herself up from the floor. The charge increased, its vibrations a powerful force taking over my body. I had no control. It was sheer instinct and an overwhelming desire to make them pay for hurting me.

But as Gerald grabbed Cordelia in a protective embrace, shock giving way to fear, a collection of photographs hanging on the wall killed my energy. There were three framed photographs spaced along the wall, each a snapshot of a family scene—Cordelia in a hospital bed, her baby swaddled in her arms. Gerald, the proud father, smiled beatifically as he gazed at the pair.

My inner power flatlined.

Another showed Gerald in the garden, dandling a toddler over a paddling pool, a young boy splashing them both. The third was Cordelia, Gerald, and the two children all dressed in matching Christmas elf pyjamas. It looked recent, perhaps this past Yule.

Gerald and I had no children. The IVF had never worked for us.

All energy drained from my body, and I staggered along the hallway. Cordelia grew bold and took a step forward. "That's right! My husband. Now get out!"

I turned, stumbled then made my way down the stairs. I have no memory of getting home.

Chapter One

Six months later

"Galahad!" My call drifted across the back garden, muted by the rolling fog. Early May in England was one of my favourite times of the year. The fog would lower and roll over the land, sparkle in the light from the rising sun, then disappear under its mist-burning heat. Today promised to be a beautiful day, but in my misery, with an unopened brown envelope in one hand, and a bowl of uneaten cat food in the other, I was oblivious to it.

"Galahad!"

There was no response, just as there had been no response for the last six weeks but, even in my depressed state, I hadn't given up. Galahad was my cat, gifted to me by Gerald after one of our rows. I'd grown tired of his endless nights away. He was on call permanently and left the house day or night claiming an emergency at work, or another broken down rig that he had to fix. He'd also begun to talk about going back to lorry driving, specifically taking freight abroad where he could earn the 'big money' as he put it. The last straw came when he had accepted a job from his old firm that would mean him being away for weeks at a time. At that point, I had no idea he was 'playing away' aka marrying another woman and raising the family we couldn't have with her, but I was already lonely and couldn't contemplate him being away for even more time. His answer was the cat, an adorable black and silver striped kitten that I'd named Sir Galahad. I'd loved him, taken what solace I could from a cat, and put up with the endless empty weeks as Gerald hauled freight around Europe. Or at least pretended to.

I had been duped. It was all a lie, and now Galahad had deserted me too!

I placed the fresh food outside the back door in the hope that if he returned whilst I was at work, at least he'd know I hadn't forgotten about him. Sometimes, the bowl would be empty, and I'd get my hopes up, but now realised it could have been any cat in the neighbourhood getting lucky with a free meal, or perhaps even rats!

After taking a final look across the mist-bound lawn in the hopes of seeing his tail rising above the fog, I closed the door.

"He's left me too." My morose tone only brought my mood lower. Flipping the switch of the kettle for my second cup of coffee, I slumped onto the kitchen chair and examined the letter. 'Baines & Simms Solicitors' was printed across the back. My heart sank a little further. This was it, the letter that ended it all, or rather confirmed the end of it all—confirmation of divorce. I took a breath and tore the envelope open before I had the chance to lose courage and unfolded the slim wad of paper. There it was, in black and white; I was a free woman. Rejected. Divorced. On the shelf. A failure!

I sighed and wandered to the kettle, made a cup of coffee then returned to read the letter, and began to sob. It was pathetic. After six months I should have just been able to shrug it off, but I was aggrieved and now even my cat had deserted me! Great heaving sobs took over my body as I began to wail.

After discovering Gerald's bigamy, my life had crumbled; the depth of his betrayal went even further than marrying another woman. He had also cleaned out our bank account, remortgaged our house leaving zero equity, and taken out a loan that I was responsible for repaying! If that wasn't bad enough, even though he had been found guilty of bigamy, he had only received a suspended sentence of three months and ordered to pay me an insulting thousand pounds in compensation. I hadn't received a penny. As of tomorrow, I would be homeless, penniless, and cat-less! Gerald still had his pristine cookie-cutter home, his orange-tanned, bleached blonde voluptuous wife, and two adoring children. I suspected that Galahad had betrayed me too and gone to live with them!

Another heaving and self-pitying sob growled its way from my belly and into the air.

Gill, my neighbour, banged on the partition wall that separated our houses. "Shurrup!" she shouted.

I gagged back the next sob, muffling it in my sleeve, wiping snot on my dressing gown. I was a pathetic mess on a downward spiral to becoming a bitter and lonely old woman. Gerald had been right to leave me! And so had Sir Galahad. I muffled another wailing sob.

From behind me came the rustle of fabric. "She's right," a woman's voice stated. "You need to shut up!"

I did not recognize the voice.

Startled by the stranger so close behind me, I jumped out of the chair. It fell with a clack. The hairs on my neck prickled as I faced the intruder then experienced a short-lived wave of relief as an elderly woman came into view. Petite to the point of tiny she was dressed in a vintage twinset, complete with pearls, thick navy stockings, and laced brogues with block heels. Around her neck was a lanyard. Her eyes were a bright green unfaded by old age. She considered me with pursed lips.

"Who the hell are you?" I managed, though my mouth had dried in an instant. My legs began to tremble as adrenaline coursed through my veins.

"Tsk! Manners."

Her response confused me. She was standing in my kitchen, uninvited, a stranger, yet I was being reprimanded. Without apology, I continued. "Who are you and what exactly are you doing in my house?"

Apart from the fact that she seemed to have wandered in off the street and into a stranger's house there was something distinctly odd about the woman. My heart pounded with a painful beat. Was she unhinged? She could be dangerous.

"A little better, but still appalling. Mind your Ps and Qs Mistress Swinson!"

She was unhinged.

She knew my name! My maiden name!

"I'm going to have to ask you to leave," I tried, unsure of how to deal with this woman. She was elderly, looked a little frail, and was perhaps an escapee from the local nursing home where they specialized in dementia patients. There was also, I remembered with a sinking sensation, a secure hospital that had begun life as an overspill prison for an asylum several miles from the town. It housed the criminally insane and there had been more than one escape in the past decade.

She shook her head. "Tsk! No, no, no! That's a terrible thing to think."

Think? I tried a different tactic, now convinced that she really was an escapee from the secure hospital or at the very least suffering some sort of dementia. The lanyard had a photograph of a young blonde woman—not the elderly woman stood in front of me. "Can I help you? Are you lost?" I reached for my phone ready to search for the local old people's home or call the police.

Her green eyes sparkled, and I caught my breath. "Your eyes ..." I shook my head as though to clear it—her eyes couldn't actually be sparkling, could they?

Her figure began to wane and became opaque. I swayed as my head began to throb and steadied myself against the table. The solidness of her form was fading before me. She wasn't real.

I sat down with a slump, covering my eyes with the palms of my hands. I was seeing things! When I opened them, she wouldn't be there. I was overwrought with emotion, suffering PTSD, imagining things! Hallucinating! Crazy old women didn't just appear magically in your kitchen, look at you with sparkling emerald eyes, then fade to become invisible.

"Mistress Swinson."

She was still there, and her voice sounded real—and demanding! I kept the palms of my hands over my eyes. I was losing the plot.

"Mistress Swinson, it is time to stop wallowing in self-pity and put the past behind you. You're needed elsewhere. Difficult times lay ahead and you're the only one who can help him."

My thoughts instantly turned to Gerald. "Him? There is no way in hell that I am going to help that lying, cheating, scumbag of a bigamist husband!" *Stop!* You're talking to an invisible woman. You're being *weird*!

"It is time to journey."

"Hah! I have no choice there," I spat, bitterness overwhelming me as I remembered that tonight was my last in this house and that the new owners were picking up the spare set of keys tomorrow morning from my solicitor. There was nothing left from the sale. Nothing left for me to build a new future.

"He needs your help," the apparition repeated.

"Go away!" I hissed. I was not going to have a conversation with an invisible woman; only crazy people did that. "Just shut up!" I whispered, head in hands. "You're not real."

"He's waiting, Leofe," the voice repeated. "They're waiting."

My head throbbed. It was all too much. I would have to make an appointment with the doctor; perhaps he could prescribe some stronger pills.

With the kitchen empty, and traumatized by the hallucination, I took a couple of herbal calmatives and showered to get ready for work. I had lost my husband, my house, my life savings, and my cat, and was clinging onto my job by a thread. With two strikes against me, I couldn't be late again.

Chapter Two

"She's got a face like a slapped arse! It's no wonder takings are down. She's putting people off. And she's late—again."

"Oh, Barry," June, my co-worker replied, "she's been through so much! That husband of hers wasn't just playing away, he married another woman."

Barry, my boss, gave an exasperated sigh. "Can't say I blame him. That Cordelia's a cracker."

"Like your women with a bit of meat do you, Baz?"

"Aye! Women should be built for comfort not for speed, in my humble opinion." Barry snorted with delight at the coarseness of his wit.

I placed my jacket on the peg, unsure whether I should confront Barry or slink away and curl up in shame under a rock. The door to the office swung open.

"Oh! It's you." Barry stood at the door, glancing from me and back into the office to June. With his unkind and coarse words overheard, he went on the offensive. "You're late! Again."

"Sorry," I said without taking my eyes from my jacket. "Traffic."

"Hah!"

It was a lame excuse; there was no traffic to speak of between my house and the garden centre, at least not enough to make me late.

"Traffic lights," I said, trying again. "They're digging up the road to lay more cables along Dungston Street. I got stuck." It was true, there were traffic lights along Dungston Street and

I had got trapped at the back of a long queue of traffic, but I hadn't left my house until two minutes before I was supposed to be at work and that was the reason I was late.

"I'll have to give you a written warning if it happens again," he said without meeting my gaze.

"I won't be late again, Barry," I said. I sounded pathetic even to myself. I should have been outraged but I'd become an emotional punch bag over the past months and this morning the stuffing was hanging out of burst seams. "Sorry."

"Right. Just get to work. Looks like there's an infestation of aphids on the roses."

"I'll mix up some-"

"Use the *Pestbeegone*."

"But that's an organophosphate."

"And?"

"Using pesticides can make aphids resistant-"

"It'll kill these buggers."

"Well, I'd prefer to use something that's not as damaging to the environment or poisonous to kids, birds, bees and-"

"You'd prefer? This is a business, Leofe. My business. Use the *Pestbeegon*e. I can't afford to lose any more plants." His tone was accusatory, as though it were my fault the plants weren't thriving.

"But-"

He held up a silencing hand and held my gaze. "The *Pestbeegone*, please."

It wasn't a request and without another word he turned on his heels and strode away, chest puffed out, belly leading.

In the office, I flipped the switch on the kettle.

"Morning, Leofe," June smiled. The base of her throat was stained pink and there was a flicker of embarrassment in her eyes. "Take no notice of him, lovie. He's a pig."

I nodded. "A perfect match for Cordelia then."

June laughed. "That's the spirit. Don't let 'em knock you down." She grabbed her gardening gloves from the counter. "I'll see you outside. There's plenty of *Pestbeegone* in the shed."

Alone in the office, I made myself a mug of tea. Every part of me railed against using the *Pestbeegone*, it was toxic, and should be banned as far as I was concerned, but Barry was the boss and this was his garden centre and it was obvious he would be quite happy to replace me, preferably with a woman with a bit of 'meat' on her bones that he could letch after.

"Bloody men," I grumbled, then, mug in hand, headed out to the potted roses to inspect the infestation.

I didn't reach the roses. Instead, I nearly choked on my tea as I took a gulp and simultaneously noticed a woman standing among the succulents. I recognized her petite frame and mop of white hair immediately. It was the imaginary woman from my kitchen, the nutter who looked like a tiny version of Miss Marple. She was there! Standing among the succulents with a magpie on her shoulder. She looked so real, eccentric, yes, but of flesh and bone. She waved and tea scalded my epiglottis. I coughed and then began to choke.

The woman was beside me in an instant. A clenched fist thumped my back.

I took a breath, coughed, and gasped once more.

More thumps, heavier now. I held up a hand for her to stop.

"There. Is it over?" The woman's green eyes were dazzling.

The pain in my back wasn't imaginary—she had thumped me hard, and more times than was necessary.

"You're real," I said whilst scanning the area for staff or customers.

"Of course."

"But in the kitchen, you disappeared. Just disappeared."

"I let myself out, dear."

"You faded away."

"You've been through a lot."

"So they keep telling me."

"Hmm. Can we talk?"

"I'm supposed to be checking for aphids."

"Oh, this is much more important than that."

She had such an earnest smile that I decided to indulge her. What harm could it do? I'd call the local nursing home later and see if they were missing an inmate.

"Go on then," I replied. "But I haven't got long."

"This is my first mission," she stated.

"Mission?"

"Yes, the Academy sent me." She held up the lanyard with the photograph of the young blonde. The name 'Murgatroyd' was written in a copperplate script beside the image.

"That's not a photo of you." I nodded at the lanyard.

"What?"

"The photo on the lanyard—it's not of you."

She frowned then turned the lanyard over. Her frown deepened. "Oh, for Thor's sake." She tapped the laminated card, and a smile replaced the frown. "There!" She turned the lanyard back to me and held it up for inspection. The passport-style photograph now showed an elderly woman with a cloud of white hair and the name Beatrice written beside the image. "The blonde was my predecessor. Just a glitch in the tech." She chuckled. "I think that's what they call it these days. All fixed now."

"So ... Beatrice ... how did you do that?"

She tapped the side of her nose. "Oh, I have many talents dear. But back to my mission. I have been sent by the Academy-"

"Academy?"

"Yes, the Academy for Advanced Witchcraft. I'm working in the Department for ... ahem ... for Delinquent ... well it's a kind of rehabilitation centre."

She really was a nutter, but I decided that the best way of dealing with her was to indulge her fantasy and then guide her to the exit.

"So why are you here, talking to me? I'm not a witch and I certainly ... I'm not a delinquent!"

"I think I've done a bad job at explaining myself."

I nodded. "I think so. I have absolutely no idea what you're talking about."

"Ah, well, I'm sure things will become clearer."

She glanced at the sky. "Time for me to go. Gilbert will look after you until the time comes."

The magpie on her shoulder chittered. She flinched.

"Not so loud, Gilbert!"

"You can't just go without explaining yourself and ... are you talking to the bird?"

"Indeed. I'm babysitting—well, he's in training." She turned to the magpie. "Gilbert, off you go!"

The bird turned to the woman, its beak poking through her cloud of white hair. She appeared to listen. "I know, but we've been given our instructions. If we don't do a good job, then it will be the last that we get offered and I, for one, am rather enjoying myself. And it's not forever."

The bird flapped its wings, eyed me whilst cocking its head, then launched itself into the air with a jump and sudden flapping of wings. It headed straight for me and, taken by surprise, I ducked whilst covering my head with my arm. The bird let out an irritated chitter.

"Hold still," demanded the woman. "Just hold out your arm and let him land."

Still crouching, I held out an arm and allowed the bird to settle on my sleeve. It chattered in a scolding fashion and eyed me with contempt.

"I don't think it likes me," I said, adding yet another animal to my list of those that seemed to find my presence offensive.

"Just do as you're told Gilbert. This is my first assignment, don't let me down."

Again, the bird burst into annoyed chattering.

"Your first job, but you're at least ... eighty."

The woman laughed. "Oh, I'm far older than that. Add another zero to that number and you'd be closer to the mark, and it's not my first job, it's my first assignment for the Academy."

"Ah," I said as though I understood. "And what exactly is your assignment?"

"To set you on your way."

"To set me on my way?"

"Yes."

"To where?"

"Oh, yes!" She withdrew a small roll of parchment from her jacket pocket. "You enjoy being in nature working with flowers and the like?"

"Yes, I always have. I have a degree in Botany."

"But you work in a garden centre?"

I gestured to the rows of tables laden with plants. "Well, yes."

"Not true," interrupted the bird.

"I ..." *Did the bird just speak?* "I do work here."

"Gilbert! You're jumping the gun there," reprimanded the woman. "Forgive Gilbert, he gets a little out of hand sometimes but as long as you feed him worms regularly then he'll be putty in your hands. Tsk! Gilbert, I'll have to tell her now. Well, the manager is going to sack you—later today."

"You can't possibly know that."

"I heard him. Well ... it is definitely what he is thinking." The bird nodded as though agreeing. I half expected it to squawk, 'I concur'. "They've had quite enough of you by all accounts and he suspects that your ... misery ... is putting people off coming here. At first it was a boon as your infamy brought in customers, but now, with profits down, he thinks they're staying away because of you."

Infamy? Is that what Gerald's betrayal has made me? Infamous? "That's rubbish!"

"He also thinks that you're preoccupied when you're here and damaging the plants. He doesn't know that it's your bad energy that's making them die – the same as the animals."

"I don't have bad energy. And I'm not killing animals!"

"No, but you are making them suffer. And yes, you do have bad energy. Green witches have that effect sometimes I'm afraid and you've been storing up the misery for so long that you've become quite toxic."

"Thanks!"

"You're welcome."

"But it's just not true. I love plants. And in any case, I'm not a witch!"

"Gilbert," she said addressing the bird. "Fetch me a fern."

Gilbert hopped from my arm and onto the table then, taking the edge of the plastic pot in his beak, lifted the small fern and flapped his way back to the woman. She held out the fern to me. "Take it."

I took the fern.

"Now, caress its leaves whilst thinking of that poor cat you've driven away."

"Sir Galahad? I haven't driven him away. Cats are free spirits. They come and go as they please."

"Yes, and he has chosen to leave. Just think of him and then perhaps throw in a few memories of Gerald and ... maybe his wife."

I shot her a look laced with the venom I felt for Cordelia. The woman flinched but remained defiant.

"Excellent. Now direct that toxic energy to the plant."

"This is crazy."

"I'm sorry to cause you pain, dear, but you'll thank me for it in the end."

"I sincerely doubt that!"

"Just touch the fern," she insisted.

I touched its leaves and, as my fingers ran along its fronds, it began to wilt then brown.

"Hah! It worked. Gilbert look. I wasn't sure, but yes, look! She's poisonous. Just poisonous."

I held the potted fern aghast. My touch *was* killing it.

"There, you see. Your energy is killing the plants."

"It's a trick. You poisoned it."

"Tsk! There are none so blind as those who refuse to see. It wasn't me that poisoned it, you did that, but don't fret dear, I'm here to help. As I said, I'm working for the Department for the Rehabilitation of Delinquent Witches. DRDW for short. Now, I really must get back."

"But-"

I bit back my words. The woman had gone, along with the magpie, and I was left alone with the desiccated fern at my feet. Wizened and brown, it lay out of its pot surrounded by scattered compost.

As I bent to retrieve the plant, I noticed the ladder leant against the old brick shed that served as the potting room. At the top, pruning shears in hand as he tackled an overgrown honeysuckle that had begun to worm its way under the pantiles, was Barry. From his slack-jawed look of disbelief it was obvious that he had overheard every word of our conversation, seen me destroy the fern, and the woman disappear. In part I was relieved; he could verify that I wasn't losing my mind.

Our eyes locked.

I tried to scramble for an explanation. "I was just talking to a customer; she wanted a fern." I scooped to pick up the disheveled plant.

"Woman?"

I gestured to where the woman had stood. "Yes, the woman. She wanted a fern." I held up the pot. A desiccated frond nodded then snapped off and fell to the ground. His eyes widened, his look one of increasing incredulity.

I placed the fern back on its table, noting the general poor health of the other plants. The leaves of the newly emerging hostas were white with mildew.

"There was no woman, Leofe!" He held my gaze.

"But she ..." I broke away from his stare. She had seemed so real! "I-"

"I think you should take the rest of the day off. Perhaps take a few days off." His eyes narrowed, there was not one iota of compassion in them. "You've been through a lot – what with the bigamy thing."

"That's all over now."

"Well, your mind ... your mind doesn't seem to be on your job. I think you should take a few days off."

"But I need the money!" I was on a zero-hours contract, so time off meant no pay.

"We'll be in touch, Leofe."

With those final words, he turned away and clipped at the honeysuckle, lopping a mass of growth before flinging it to the ground. He wasn't just pruning the honeysuckle—he was butchering it. And, just like the roadside hedges that were cut back and left mutilated, torn, and ragged in the autumn, I hated to see it.

"But, Barry, I need the money!"

Pretending to ignore me, he continued to hack at the honeysuckle throwing another part of the vine on the growing pile beside the shed. By the time he had finished it would be a stump, no longer a refuge for the birds that nested among its leaves.

My cheeks prickled and grew warm. "Right," I muttered. "I'll go then."

Barry didn't answer and gave the vine another vicious snip. "There's a bird's nest in there!"

More leaves and vines with their clusters of bright red berries fell, adding to the pile. "There's a wren that lives ..." I groaned as the last of the leaves was mercilessly lopped. It was pointless, the vine was now a stump. My anger boiled. "I hope you fall off that ladder!" I said with feeling and turned to walk away.

Ignored and dismissed, sure that Barry would give out the word not to offer me any more hours - a zero-hours contract meant zero work as and when they pleased - I tramped back towards the office, anger giving way to resignation. I hadn't walked more than ten feet before a man's scream, accompanied by the screech of splintering wood, stopped me in my tracks. I turned to the noise to see the ladder yawing away from the shed, Barry still at its top. The angle increased, Barry grasped at the honeysuckle to try and bring it back into place but in a moment of pure karma, the damaged vine snapped, and the ladder twisted on its feet. My relief as the ladder and Barry swung back towards the shed was short lived as they continued to twist then began a slow-motion journey away from the shed and crashed to the ground.

Chapter Three

With the bike locked away in the garage, and the door slammed shut behind me, I unscrewed the top of the bottle of wine I'd bought on the way home and took a swig.

My stomach growled but ignoring the need for real food, I took a larger gulp of wine, and grabbed the sharing bag of crisps and four pack of chocolate bars I had also purchased. I had no intention of behaving and was going to indulge my misery by stuffing my face with junk and getting drunk.

I was scared.

I had nothing. No man, no money, no home and, to top it all, I was losing my mind.

I took another swig from the bottle. Catching sight of myself in the kitchen window brought my efforts at getting drunk to an immediate halt. Over the past months, I had lost weight to the point of thinness and with my hair pulled back in an unkempt and unflattering ponytail, the bottle held up to my mouth, I looked one step away from being a homeless and alcoholic wreck. No wonder my colleagues kept giving me funny looks and Barry wanted me gone; I was in a state.

Something inside snapped.

The disheveled, definitely-looking-middle-aged-in-a-scrawny-kind-of-way woman staring back at me in the glass was not who I wanted to be!

"Oh, mum," I said, suddenly bereft. "I wish you were here."

I felt her absence like a pain. She would never have let me get into such a state.

"She is here." The voice spoke softly and with compassion. "She's inside you—always."

The hairs on my neck crept. It was her again! The imaginary woman. I swivelled to the voice, but the room was empty. I was experiencing an auditory hallucination, something I knew was a sign of schizophrenia. 'Visions' were something my beloved mother had struggled with throughout my childhood and were only kept at bay with medication.

"You are not real!" I exclaimed, my heart beating hard, now seriously concerned for my mental health. "You are not real."

The next voice I heard was my mother's, but this one didn't cause fear. It was a memory, a remembered conversation. 'You're only a victim if you allow them to make you one. You're strong, Leofe, so much stronger than you realise.'

"Oh, mum!" I leant back against the sink and then something clicked inside, as though a switch had been flicked on. "You're right! And I'm not going to be a victim anymore."

Turning to the sink, I upended the bottle and held it over the plughole until it was empty. I was not going to get drunk, and I was not going to binge on the extra-large bag of crisps and four-pack of chocolate bars I'd bought along with the wine either.

I began to consider the hallucination. The woman wasn't real, obviously, but was my subconscious trying to tell me something? I wasn't poisonous, it was ridiculous to believe that I could actually make a frond crumble just by touching it, but my energy was toxic, and it was poisoning me. Although, I remembered, the plants at the nursery had been struggling lately; we'd had an outbreak of rust on the snapdragons, slime flux on the clematis, and black death in the hellebores. I turned my hands over, could I really destroy plants with my touch? Perhaps I should try it out in the garden.

"No!" I clenched my fists tight. "It's all just nonsense. The woman is not real. You do not have the power to destroy plants, and you are not a witch."

But mother had many talents. She saw things. She always knew how to make things better. Remember the poultice she put on your ankle? Remember how swollen and purple it was? You were in agony, but within an hour it was as good as new.

"I misremembered. Exaggerated."

Mother saw things, talked to invisible people too.

She struggled with her mental health! That's all.

Or perhaps she had the gift?

"No! There's no such thing." The neighbour's voice, heard through the partition wall as she began to harangue her husband, made me cautious of speaking and I pressed my lips together, aware I was talking to myself. I was being *weird*! If I could hear them, they could hear me too. I checked my watch. Twelve-thirty. Craig, her husband, was home from work and her badgering had begun like clockwork. I felt sorry for the poor man. No sooner had he stepped through the door than she would start on him. Why did he stay? If I'd been easier to deal with perhaps Gerald wouldn't have gone?

Stop it!

My head began to ache with the rollercoaster of my thoughts.

The leaves turned brown. She said that you were toxic.

"I'm not a witch," I muttered. "That's just ridiculous"

Is it? Don't you remember when Allan Gradgrind threw those stones at you? He was calling you a witch even then. You made him fall over in that muddy puddle.

No! I don't remember.

"You're talking to yourself again. Stop it. And you're not going mad. You've just been through a lot," I whispered.

My stomach growled with hunger but without cooking utensils, fridge, or food, I was faced with the bag of crisps and bars of chocolate. At that moment, I decided to leave the house, staying would only be a way of punishing myself even more.

Pulling the phone from my back pocket I called the Bed & Breakfast to book myself in for the night. They had a room available and could recommend a local pub that guests said served homemade meals.

Later that evening, sat on the narrow bed at the B&B, I began my search for a new job, certain that my zero-hour contract at the garden centre would be terminated. I must have muttered about the ladder louder than I realized because Barry had flinched as I'd approached him and told June what I'd said. She had cast me a wary sideways glance but told him not to be silly, and that she'd already told him that very morning to go steady pruning the honeysuckle.

'She's a witch or something,' he'd spat. 'I saw her, I saw the plant go brown beneath her fingers. She was talking to herself, casting *spells* and then the frond went brown and crumbled. There was a magpie on her arm too! I saw it with my own eyes!'

'Oh, Barry! There's no such thing as witches.' June turned to me. 'Did he hit his head when he fell?'

I'd mumbled that he had. She'd sighed and turned back to the injured man.

'The plants aren't doing well, Barry, because they've not been properly watered.'

'And that's her fault too!'

June had come to my defence. 'Well, the poor love has been through the wringer.'

'Yeah, and now her slapped-arse face is driving away my customers.'

With Barry being tended to by June, and with no evidence of broken bones or other damage, I'd left him chuntering, certain that I wouldn't be welcome back.

I sighed, found an online job site and, unsure quite what to search for, typed in 'gardener'. I left the distance open as there was nothing to keep me in this area and hit 'search'. The app informed me that there were over one thousand results for job adverts containing the word 'gardener'. I made a coffee, then settled back on the bed to scroll through the list. Despite the strain of the day, a ripple of excitement ran through me. I had cut the cord. I was free to do whatever I wanted. This was the start of a new adventure – if I could keep my sanity in check.

Chapter Four

I began to scroll through the list of jobs. There were a few interesting ones, but the majority were for people looking for someone to mow lawns or tidy their gardens. I wanted more. If I could move anywhere in the country, then I wasn't going to be weeding flower beds for old ladies. I had the qualifications – a first class degree in Botany from the University of Birmingham, numerous certificates from the Royal Horticultural Society, and several years as Birmingham's Botanical Gardens' Assistant Head Gardener gained before we moved for Gerald's work. I'd only taken the job at Barry's place after being made redundant from my last job as nursery manager. The plant nursery's tea rooms, potting shed, and shop had burned down in a devastating fire, and the owner had decided she'd had enough of the English weather and moved to join her daughter and grandchild in Australia once the insurance money had been paid out.

"Come on, Leofe! From now on, life is going to be an adventure."

I typed 'Head Gardener' into the search bar. The search returned seventy-three jobs. The first was working for the council in Tower Hamlets, London. *Grim!* "Nope," I said and flicked through to the next job. The second was for a landscape gardener with a design firm—interesting but not really what I wanted. It was the third that really caught my attention and I sat bolt upright, incredulous.

"Yes! No way! Yes!"

The advert read,

Estate & Poison Garden Manager

Blackwood Hall, Northumberland

The Estate Manager's role is based here at our Stately Home located in Northumberland. This is a live-in role, that comes with a spacious apartment within the house and includes all utility bills.

To be successful in this role, you will need a thorough understanding of all aspects of grounds and estate maintenance duties, knowledge of working within a conservation area, excellent communication skills, a customer focused approach, sound decision making skills and the ability to work well under pressure.

This is a full-time role with normal working hours, although there may be a requirement to work outside of standard business hours at certain times, including weekends and holidays and bank holidays.

Key Responsibilities

Responsibility for the maintenance and upkeep of all 42 acres of garden areas including paths to a high standard including regular mowing, hedge cutting, topiary, and with special responsibility for the Poison Garden ...

The advert continued and I read it with increasing excitement. There was nothing on the list of duties that I could not fulfil. I checked the person specification. I ticked all the boxes there too. It was the perfect job for me. I was the perfect candidate. And – oh, joy of joys! – it was an historic garden in Northumberland, my absolute favourite area of England. I had so many happy memories of holidays there with my mother. I had always wanted to work somewhere beautiful, and you couldn't get more beautiful than a stately home. The poison garden element sounded intriguing too. I'd been entranced by the one at Alnwick Castle on a visit years ago and hoped that this one was similar.

I read on – 'salary to be discussed at interview. Immediate start.' A bar at the bottom of the advert read, 'Click here for interview'. With an immediate start plus accommodation in a 'spacious apartment' within the main house, it was an opportunity I could not miss. There was no option to upload a CV for consideration. This was it! I could attend an interview tomorrow—any day. High on a wave of determination to live a new and different life, I clicked the button.

Several fields appeared for my name and contact number. I filled them in and then clicked 'Book Interview'. The screen grew blank and then, to my horror, a face appeared on the screen and an older woman with intense green eyes, soft pink lips, and white hair cut short, smiled back at me. Despite her age, my guess was that she was around seventy years old, her delicately boned face was unlined, her skin clear, and her eyes bright with intelligence.

"Good evening, Leofe. Thank you for contacting us. Are you able to go ahead with the interview?"

"Now?"

The woman nodded. "Yes, that would be preferable."

Taken by surprise, I agreed, too flustered to consider whether this was yet another hallucination.

The woman waited patiently as I composed myself, introduced herself as Aelfwen, then began to ask a series of questions that I assumed were just to help me feel more at ease but amounted to nothing more than reciting what my qualifications were and what jobs I'd had. She smiled and nodded and praised me. I waited for the punch—the question that was meant to trip me up or really dig into my past, but it didn't come, and I spent several minutes talking about the skills I'd acquired over the years and the different gardens I'd worked in.

"Now, Leofe" she said after I'd explained that I was currently working in a local garden centre but was looking for new challenges, "there is one item that most of our poison gardeners have had and that's a special book where they collect their notes and write down their knowledge gathered over the years. Do you have such a book?"

I didn't. I had folders that contained my notes and essays from my university days and the various courses I had taken over the years, but they were all in storage. I stalled, a sense of failure already descending.

"They're often full of herbal recipes, how to make tinctures, that kind of thing," she smiled encouragingly.

"Why, yes! I do," I said, hope returning as I remembered my mother's herbal, the only item I'd allowed myself to keep out of storage. "I do have a book like that."

"Wonderful. Please bring it with you."

Ah, so, this was just a preliminary interview. I was unlikely to make it past the next stage. "Yes, sure."

"Good. Well, that concludes our interview. I'll send you an email with directions to the Hall. Welcome to the team. We shall expect you after luncheon."

Stunned, I remained silent for several moments. "Does that mean I got the job?"

She nodded. "Indeed it does, Mistress Swinson. You're more than perfect for the role. Indeed, I would say it was made for you." Her smiling face faded, and the screen became blank.

Luncheon! Mistress Swinson? There was something archaic about the way the woman spoke. Hadn't the woman who'd appeared in my kitchen called me the same?

Life was becoming increasingly peculiar.

I paced the room, swinging from elation to disbelief. I had a job! Not just any job. The perfect job. One that I had dreamed of for what seemed like forever.

And then doubt set in as memories of Gerald's exasperated face surfaced; 'You'll never be able to do it, Leofe', 'You're an idiot, Leofe. What makes you think you're up to the job?', 'He's only taking you on because he's got the hots for you'. Years of derogatory remarks from my now ex-husband had taken their toll and my newly found enthusiasm for embracing the future began to wane. What if it hadn't been real? What if I'd imagined it all—just like I'd imagined the woman? Had I imagined the interview? Was this another hallucination? It had seemed so real, but so had the woman who told me I was toxic, and Barry hadn't seen her. My head throbbed.

Stop this nonsense. Gerald demeaned you to make sure you didn't question him. He's a bigamist and a liar. He controlled you for years but now you are free. Believe in yourself again.

Battered by seesawing thoughts, I boiled the kettle and chose a sachet of hot chocolate from the courtesy basket. The kettle boiled and I covered the powder with water. As I stirred the powder to a paste a notification alerted me to an email. Hot chocolate in hand, I sat on the bed and checked the message. It was from Blackwood Hall with detailed directions of how to get there.

"It *is* real!" *Surreal perhaps, but real.*

Chapter Five

I woke in the morning to the sound of voices in the hallway and a bright stream of morning light bursting through the gap left by the badly fitted curtains. Disorientated, I listened to the voices for several semi-conscious moments wondering who was in my house. Seconds passed and then I remembered. I was not at home, I was in a hotel bedroom, and I started my new job today!

Today!

Flinging off the bedcovers, heart now pounding, I sprang out of bed. I was late! The sun was already strong enough to warm my cheeks and I had to be at Blackwood Hall 'after luncheon', a hard three-hour ride at the very least. I staggered to the ensuite, my fifty-one-year-old knees and attached tendons complaining loudly that they needed a little more time to warm up before being abused, then stepped into the shower before it had time to warm up.

The shock of cold water sloughed off any remaining sluggishness and I showered then dressed in record time, stomach growling with hunger. I checked my watch. It was already a quarter to ten.

After reading the email from Blackwood Hall for the umpteenth time just to reassure myself that it was real, I had checked the route. Driving up to Northumberland would take four hours, but on the bike, if I rode hard, I could cut that down to about three. With no time to stop for breakfast, or even have a cup of tea in the bedroom, I downed a glass of water, packed my bag, and made my way to reception to return the key.

A large ginger and white cat lay curled on an overstuffed chair in the hallway, warmed in the pool of light flooding through the glass doors. It eyed me with disinterest as I took the final step down the stairs but as I stepped closer to the reception desk, it moved to a crouch, its ears flat against its head. It hissed as I placed the keys on the desk.

"Everything alright for you, Miss?" the young girl behind the counter asked. She had a pleasant, well-trained smile.

"Yes, thank you," I replied.

"I'm afraid you've missed breakfast."

Behind me the cat growled.

"I was late up," I explained with a sigh, reminded of the ache in my belly.

The cat continued to growl. The girl threw it a concerned glance and as I turned to look, it hissed.

"Stop that, Jemima!" She wagged a finger at the cat. "I'm sorry, she doesn't usually do that."

The cat continued to growl, staring directly at me and, as I took a step towards the door, stood on all fours and arched its back, fangs revealed in a snarl.

"Jemima!"

The cat was huge, its form made more impressive by fur now standing on end, back arched, ears flat against its head.

I froze, sure that the huge cat was about to attack.

"Whatever is the matter, Jemima?" The girl stepped out from behind the counter and scooped up the cat with an impressive show of fearlessness.

I breathed a sigh of relief and stepped towards the door. The cat yowled but made no effort to move as the girl held it in her arms. "Shush now, silly!" she cooed, glanced at me perplexed, and nodded towards the door—my cue to leave.

Outside, I welcomed the sun's warmth on my face. The cat's reaction was disturbing, another peculiar incident to add to the list. Apart from Sir Galahad's disappearance, I had noticed that dogs were becoming increasingly noisy around me. Until now, I'd dismissed it as foolishness on my part for even thinking it was personal but, after this morning, I began to wonder if perhaps it was. Add to that the bird incident when I was pegging out the washing the other week, then Beatrice's insistence that I was toxic was perhaps closer to the truth than I wanted to accept.

However, now was not the time to ponder why animals seemed to have taken against me and I packed my luggage into the bike's paniers, pulled on my helmet and gloves, straddled the seat, and started the engine. It growled into life.

Biking was a joy, and I navigated the busy roads through town with growing anticipation until I reached the open road. There were only several miles of road through the countryside until I hit the motorway, but I enjoyed every winding second as the bike clung to the road and I leaned into the curves. It was freedom and I left the town, and the house I'd shared with Gerald for seventeen of our thirty years together, without a backward glance or single ounce of regret.

A new chapter of my life was about to unfold. The story ahead was unknown and that was terrifying. It was also exhilarating, but if I'd known what lay ahead, I may not have motored north that day.

An hour later, the pain of hunger making my stomach roil with nausea, I turned into a motorway service station and pulled up beside a cart selling 'homemade' Cornish pasties. I ordered a traditional pasty - anything else was heresy, and the curried ones an abomination – and a cup of tea, then seated myself at one of the small tables. Despite making good time, I couldn't afford to take long and bit into the pasty taking a large, unladylike bite.

"Tsk! Manners."

I recognized the voice immediately. Beatrice. The imaginary woman who had appeared in my kitchen and then at work. Startled, a large chunk of barely chewed pasty caught at the back of my throat, and I spent the next seconds coughing. Once again, her hand pounded my back. My throat cleared, and I took a sip of tea. Newly poured into the cardboard beaker, it scalded my lips and tongue. The hand slapped my back once again, and scalding tea spilled across the table. Tea dripped over the edge of the table.

"You alright, love?" The vendor leant forward. "You need something?"

"Scalded!" I rasped.

"I'll get you some water."

The woman sat opposite, back straight, green eyes fixed on me as the vendor brought a bottle of water and a wad of serviettes to mop up the spilt tea. "On the house," he said. "I should have warned you the pasties come out on the hot side."

The tip of my tongue and lips tingling with pain, I gratefully accepted the water. "Thanks," I managed.

He made no sign that he'd seen the woman at the table as he mopped at the spilt tea. I took a swig of water, allowing it to bathe my tongue. My lips burned.

"Take your time, dear," she said then frowned as she leaned forward. "Ooh! I think that may blister."

I ignored her as I poured cold water on a wadded serviette and pressed it to my burning lips. There was no way I was going to respond to an invisible woman whilst out in public—even in private I would ignore this figment of my imagination.

"I have salve. It will clear that up right away." She reached inside her pocket and placed a small silver tin on the table. A design of flowers was pressed into the metal. It looked surprisingly real, but I continued to ignore her. "It'll help. I promise."

My mind was really doing a job on me! She looked so real, and the tin had even clinked as she'd placed it onto the table, but the vendor had paid her no attention.

"Leofe?"

"Donna maleduccata," the vendor muttered and, despite my lack of fluency in Italian, I recognized his words; 'Rude woman'!

In the next moment, he was beside the table. "Can I get you anything to drink, lady?"

"How kind!" Beatrice replied. "A cup of tea would be lovely, thank you." She smiled with thanks at the man, and he returned to his cart to prepare the tea.

"She's real," I whispered. "But she can't be."

"Well, of course I am."

"But Barry couldn't see you. He thought I was talking to myself."

She giggled. "I know. It was naughty of me."

"Naughty!"

"Yes, and did you see him fall?" She cackled then covered her mouth to muffle the noise. "I know we shouldn't laugh, but ... well, he was really rather horrid to you."

I nodded. "I've never really liked him, to be honest."

"Well, I'm sure you'll like your new boss a whole lot better." She raised her brows in a meaningful glance.

"The new job? How do you know about that?"

The vendor brought the woman's tea to the table. She delved into a worn leather purse and handed over a five-pound note. We waited in silence until he'd returned her change. She blew at the tea before sipping it with care.

"Do use the salve," she said gesturing to the tin with her free hand. "It will reduce the swelling."

I touched my lips with a delicate finger. The skin felt hot and tight. "Has it blistered?"

She nodded. "The salve is made with aloe. It will help but use it sooner rather than later."

I shook my head. "No, it's okay, thanks. I've got some lip balm."

"But this will-"

"No, it's okay. I'm sorted, thanks."

She shrugged her shoulders in surrender. "As you like. But ... well, I hope they heal quickly."

"I'm sure they will," I replied, instantly regretting the smile I offered as the burning sensation intensified.

I should have accepted gracefully but instead I checked my watch and stood to leave, confused by the encounter. I had been sure this eccentric woman had been a figment of my imagination, but now it seemed that I was wrong. But if she was real, how had she found me?

"Are you ... following me?"

"Why yes, dear. Of course."

"You're stalking me? Who's paying you? Is it Gerald?"

"Well, I'd rather not speak of it here. There are mice at the crossroads." She gestured to the vendor. He caught my glance and quickly turned away and made a pretence of tidying the stacks of cardboard beakers.

"Mice?"

"Yes," she cast a meaningful glance towards the vendor. "At the crossroads."

"You mean he's listening?"

She sighed. "Yes, exactly that."

"Ah. So, you don't want him to know that you're working for the Academy of Advanced Witchcraft?"

She frowned, glanced over at the vendor, and shook her head at me in silent disapproval.

"Oh, what a silly thing to say," she laughed, pushed the lanyard beneath her jacket and took a sip of her tea. "There's no such thing."

I checked my watch, confused by her presence and the conversation. Right now, I had to focus on getting up to Blackwood Hall. I wanted to make a good impression and arriving late was not the way to do it.

Still unsure if I was imagining the entire encounter, I turned my back to the vendor. "If you'll excuse me, I don't want to be rude, but I have to get going."

"I understand, dear, but don't sign the contract without me being there."

I shook my head. None of this made sense and the last thing I wanted, after finally freeing myself of the emotional burden of Gerald and his controlling ways, was to allow anyone to interfere with my business. I wouldn't be controlled again.

"I'm sure I can manage to read a contract." I kept my voice low. "Thanks all the same."

"No, I must insist-"

Insist? "Thanks. Listen, I don't understand what's going on. You may be a figment of my imagination for all I know, but I won't be told what to do anymore. Not by you. Not by Gerald. Not by anyone."

She shook her head. "Have it your way."

"I will," I said in quiet defiance.

Her shoulders sagged. Remorse nudged me. "I don't mean to be rude ... I'm ... Oh, heck! I have no idea what's going on, but I do know that if I don't get back on that bike, I'm going to be late for a job I just can't mess up."

"Well, that is a concern, you are a Swinson after all."

Close by a dog began to yap.

"And I think you're right about leaving," she said as the dog's yapping grew louder. "Sooner rather than later."

The dog yelped as its owner tugged at its lead. "Give over, you daft dog!" Undeterred, the tiny dog, a smooth-haired chihuahua, strained forward, a vicious gleam in its eyes, and yapped.

As the man tugged at the dog, dragging it along the path and away from me, I returned to my bike, leaving the woman to finish her tea, and made my way north to Blackwood Hall.

Chapter Six

Endless motorway stretched beyond the horizon and for another two hours I focused on the road ahead until eventually reaching the junction that would take me to the smaller winding road that led to Blackwood Hall. My lower back ached and though I yearned to pull to the side of the road and take a few minutes to stretch out my legs, I continued along increasingly narrow and winding lanes until I reached the final turn off.

The road had taken me higher and into a dense area of woodland where a narrow lane cut through the hillside. Earth pushed against low stone walls that bowed under the pressure whilst above sunlight filtered through a thickening spring canopy. After travelling for hours along the motorway, passing gargantuan warehouses, flanked by lorries and speeding cars with engines roaring, travelling along the lane was like being in a different world. It *was* a different world and one that soothed the soul.

Ahead, a break in the stone wall was marked by two stone pillars. Carved into one, the letters greened by lichen, was 'Blackwood Hall Estate'. Beside it, almost hidden by this year's new growth, a weathered sign read 'Poison Garden' in a calligraphic script. Below it read 'Tea Room'. A red arrow painted beside the titles pointed skyward. A skull and cross bones had been painted in black at the bottom corner.

If the owners were hoping to attract visitors to the garden, then they had a lot to learn. Other gardens I'd worked for had signage placed miles from the attraction and usually huge and well-kept signs at the entrance. This place was doing a poor job of advertising. Perhaps they relied on word of mouth?

I turned into the entrance and passed through the pillars then braked as a wave of energy passed over me. Surprised, I stalled the engine. The tingling sensation wasn't painful but nor was it pleasant and I shuddered as though chilled, then scanned the entrance for evidence of anything that could be emitting an electrical charge but could see nothing among the overgrown shrubs that hugged the pillars. Nor were there any cables lying along the ground, threaded through the shrubs and ferns, or hung through the trees. There was no sign of security cameras or anything that could have caused the surge of electrical energy that passed through me either.

Disconcerted by the sensation, but keen to reach the house, I restarted the engine and continued along the driveway. It was a slow process. Like the lanes that brought me to the estate boundary, the driveway was long and winding. It also descended at a far steeper rate than it had risen and was rutted by tyre marks and potted with huge and muddy puddles filled with last autumn's rotting leaves. Despite riding slowly, my leathers became spattered with mud and my temperature rose with the effort of weaving around the puddles. With a final burst of speed, I rounded the last puddle and emerged from the woodland driveway a hot, sweaty, and dirty mess. I was also late. I hadn't been given a specific time to arrive but guessed that three pm was not exactly 'after luncheon'.

Before me sat a magnificent house.

Built of dark grey stone, it rose from the land like a gothic castle. It filled the open space between the trees that hugged it so that access was limited to the grand entrance or one of several heavy doors set into the stone walls that flanked either side. There were numerous enormous and arched mullioned windows along the frontage. Wide stone steps led to a heavy door reached through a stone archway with side pillars topped by a pair of winged and frowning grotesques. Either side sat vast urns each with a topiary cut to a spiral shape but in need of clipping. Ivy grew around the door and above the window beside it.

A gravelled driveway circled a stone fountain with a lowcut boxwood hedge that had begun to grow wild and, like the spiral topiary, lose its clipped shape. A sign with 'car park' painted in black lettering was accompanied by a red arrow that pointed towards a gap in the hedge. Gargoyles sat at the corners, their mouths open and ready to spout rainwater from the guttering, watched as I rode past to the carpark. A hopeful sign read 'overspill carpark' and pointed to a field overgrown with grass beyond a tall and sprouting hedge of privet.

I cut the engine, flipped out the stand, and dismounted, relieved to pull my helmet off. A fresh breeze caught in my hair, cooling my overheated scalp. A bead of sweat dribbled down my temple. Another helpful sign pointed me in the direction of the 'Gardens' and after swapping my helmet for my bag, I made my way to the closed gate, presuming that, as the place was open to the public, I would find a washroom and freshen up. After riding for over four hours – the winding route after the motorway had taken far longer than I'd anticipated – I was a mess. There was no way I could meet my future boss in this state!

A heavy, ironwork gate supported by stone pillars and flanked by overgrown privet hedging was the entrance to the garden. To my relief, it was unlocked, and the latch clicked up without any ominous creaking. The hinges were well-oiled, so someone was looking after the place despite the neglected air of the shrubbery and signage I'd noticed so far. Stepping through the gate led me to a path of stone slabs, again hedged in by privet that was over eight feet tall and hadn't been clipped for some time, at least not at the end of last season. The new season's growth was already intruding into the narrow space and caught my sleeves as I followed the path. The gate disappeared as the path curved and then curved again. I hurried my steps, beginning to feel hemmed in and lost. As reality began to take on a surreal air, the narrow pathway widened, and I found myself in front of an arched doorway. Either side were shrubs for several feet. This was the only way forward. I stepped into the narrow space and grasped the heavy ring of barley-twist metal that served as a door handle. Beyond was a spacious courtyard.

Many stately and country homes that had opened their doors to the public had converted their outbuildings into cafes, shops, restaurants, wedding venues, and workshops, but these buildings looked unspoiled, slightly dilapidated and with their original use unchanged. On the far side were a series of stable doors, one with its top half open, a large chestnut horse stared at me with interest then whinnied and backed into its stable.

On the other side of the courtyard a door opened revealing a passageway and the garden beyond and the trees beyond that. The advert had stated that the estate covered forty-two acres and I began to realise just how large the job I had taken on was. My heart skipped a beat and I swallowed down the panic that was beginning to rise. I had set off with such confidence. Such resolve for this to be a new start, a new adventure, but here I was, a bedraggled mess wandering around like a clueless visitor. I should have stopped earlier to freshen up.

A young woman walked through the door and into the courtyard and waved.

I waved back and stood as though caught in headlights as she drew closer. Dressed in an oversized jumper and dungarees, the legs tucked into flower-patterned wellington boots, hair hidden beneath a headscarf tied at the front in a knot, she reminded me of a waif-like Rosie the Rivetter. Slender with delicate bone structure and flaxen hair, violet eyes, outlined by dark lashes, sparkled. As she caught my gaze she smiled. I could only stare back, caught by the sparkle in her eyes. It was an odd sensation; I felt held in time.

She took a step forward and wrinkled her nose in distaste. "Oh! Are you the new gardener?" she asked and took a step back, holding a slender finger beneath her nose. It was a momentary reaction, but one I couldn't mistake. Mortification began to bloom in my cheeks; not only was I hot and sweaty, but from the girl's reaction, I must smell too. "We were expecting you earlier," she stated, still holding my gaze.

I found it impossible to look away; the sparkle in her eyes was drawing me in, trapping me. "I ... it took me a lot longer than I hoped to get here," I said. "I was hoping to freshen up before I-"

"Jodi!" A woman's voice called from across the courtyard.

The girl blinked and although her eyes were still a striking violet colour they no longer sparkled. Suddenly released, I caught sight of the woman calling from across the courtyard. It was Aelfwen, the woman who had interviewed me last night. Far taller than I had imagined, she was slender, and dressed from head to toe in black. Elegant in a slim-fitting skirt, she wore a fine-knit polo neck sweater and an unbuttoned fitted jacket of black wool. A string of pearls and a pair of pearl drop earrings finished the outfit. Her short-cropped hair was perfect for her pixie-like features. She bore a striking resemblance to the much younger girl stood before me although Aelfwen's eyes were a bright green, not unlike the imaginary/not imaginary woman stalking me. Remembering her, I scanned the court-yard, relieved that she was nowhere in sight.

"Mistress Swinson!" Aelfwen was suddenly beside Jodi her hand held out.

I took the offered hand. "Yes, I guess. Although you can call me Leofe."

Aelfwen nodded. "Leofe."

I nodded and offered a smile. Aelfwen wrinkled her nose, and the faintest expression of distaste passed over her face. She could smell me too!

"I was hoping to freshen up," I said, now increasingly flus-tered. "That's why I didn't come to the front door."

"She stinks!" Jodi stated.

"Hey!" I said, shocked at the girl's rudeness.

"Jodi!" Aelfwen reprimanded.

The horse reappeared at the stable door, whinnied then pawed at the ground. The scrape of metal against stone cobbles rang out.

"She does, though. Maurice wouldn't even come into the courtyard and Cosimo is getting het up. Look at him." She ges-tured to the horse, still whinnying and pawing at the cobbled stable floor.

"Maurice is a coward," stated Aelfwen.

Jodi cocked her head and narrowed her eyes. "Don't let him hear you saying that."

"It's true. He is." Aelfwen said without remorse.

"Is there anywhere I can freshen up. I know I'm a little-"

"Pungent?"

"Well, a little-"

"Stenchy?"

"Well ... stenchy is not even a word!" I retorted becoming increasingly annoyed at the young woman's attitude.

"It is now," she smiled, her eyes once more sparkling.

I was overwhelmed by the need to agree with her and was about to reply when Aelfwen stepped between us. "Jodi!" she reprimanded. "Cease and desist."

The girl chuckled. "Sorry, Aelfwen."

"Now, where were we."

"I wanted to freshen up."

"She does stink though."

Aelfwen sighed. "Jodi!"

"Well, she does. She's toxic."

"I am not!"

"You are."

The horse whinnied.

"Listen to poor Cosimo. He's desperate to get away."

"I do not smell that badly! I may have a little B. O. but-"

"Oh, dear, it's not that you smell. What Jodi meant is that you're toxic. Poisonous."

"How dare you!"

"Now, now. Don't get overexcited. We're here to help. You must have noticed how the animals react to you? Cosimo for example," she gestured to the horse who was now rearing up and banging his hooves on the door. "Tsk! Stop that, Cosimo," Aelfwen shouted. "You'll do yourself an injury." She turned to the girl. "Go and soothe him, Jodi. Tell him to be patient."

Jodi agreed and walked over to the horse.

"Now, let's talk, dear," Aelfwen said, turning to me. "Somewhere downwind of Cosimo."

Too shocked to respond, I followed her across the courtyard.

Chapter Seven

On the other side of the courtyard, opposite the now still horse, Aelfwen opened a door and ushered me through.

"This is our shop," she said gesturing to the shelves that lined the brick wall. The shelves were bare but for a few dust-covered boxes. Cobwebs loaded and dark with dust hung in loops across the whitewashed walls. The air was fusty with undertones of earth. I shivered in the cool air. "The shop is one of the things we'd like your help with."

"Oh, I thought I was to be Head Gardener?"

"Oh, yes, you are," she replied, "with especial interest in the Poison Garden, but the shop comes under your remit too. It was in the job description."

I didn't recall reading about the shop in the description but didn't want to rock the boat by disagreeing with her.

"Jodi will be your assistant. We hope that you'll manage the shop whilst she runs it."

"Okay ..."

"Well, you'll decide what to buy, which plants to stock in here etcetera etcetera and so forth and Jodi can serve the customers ... and whatever else is necessary."

"Customers?" There was a lot of work to be done before the shop would be ready for customers. "When does the Hall open to visitors?"

"Oh ... well it's always open."

"And do you have many visitors?"

"Well ... no, but we're hoping to change that." She turned to me with a beaming smile. "Now that you're here. The marketing, the advertising—you can be in charge of all of that."

A knot of dread formed in my stomach; marketing a business was beyond my comfort zone. "But that's not really my expertise."

"Oh, well, I know that you'll manage," she said with a confidence that I felt sure, no knew, was misplaced. "Now, enough of this chatter—I'll show you around the Hall and gardens later and explain all of your duties, what we really must address is the problem at hand."

"That I'm poisonous?"

She nodded.

"Seriously? Come on! I know that I may be a little sweaty from the journey, but poisonous?"

"The animals?" she shrugged as if that explained everything.

"So, a few dogs have barked at me recently. How does that make me poisonous?"

"Your cat?"

"Sir Galahad? How do you know about him?" My mind churned. The woman was odd. The situation was odd. But I just couldn't figure out quite what was wrong. "Is this some sort of prank? I've been set up, haven't I." It was the only logical explanation. Someone who knew me had set me up to make me look a fool. It was elaborate, brilliant even, but it was all fake. It would all be filmed and uploaded to social media, and I'd be a laughingstock.

Aelfwen shook her head as I checked the walls for any signs of a hidden camera, poking my fingers through a gap where the ceiling and wall met.

"No, no, Leofe. It's not like that."

Jodi appeared in the doorway. "She doesn't know, does she."

Aelfwen shook her head. "No, it would appear that she is an innocent."

"I'm guilty of nothing!" I retorted still looking for any object that could hide a camera. "You can't catch me out. I've done nothing wrong." There was nothing hidden in the gap, and neither woman held a mobile phone that could be secretly recording.

"How can she not know?"

"Cognitive dissonance, dear. Plus, her mother didn't tell her."

"But surely Beatrice-"

"This is Bea's first time. We shall cut her a little slack, as the modern folk say."

"Excuse me," I said, "but I am still here."

"Ah, yes, sorry, Leofe. Jodi is just a little surprised at your lack of ... shall we call it self-awareness?"

I had a sudden realization and knew exactly why I was emitting a foul odour that was upsetting the animals. "If you're on about me being poisonous again, that is just utter rubbish. I know exactly why the horse doesn't like me, it's because it finds my smell offensive."

"It does," Jodi agreed with far more sincerity than was polite.

"Yes, and that's because I used a new perfume this morning."

"Perfume?"

"Oh, dear. This is going to be far harder that I thought; she really is in denial."

"Yes!" I stated. "It was a Christmas gift, from my ex. I should have binned it, but it looked expensive, and he's taken enough from me already." That morning I'd sprayed myself with some perfume Gerald had bought me for Christmas. I had wondered whether it was fake. Now I was sure—the cheap, lying, cretinous-

Aelfwen held up a hand as though warding me off. "Try to think happier thoughts, dear. I'm rather getting a headache."

I had a headache of my own and was beginning to feel emotional; here I was again, being made to feel small and stupid and confused and I'd had a gutful of that. "So am I!" I stated. "I came here to work, not be insulted." I zipped up my jacket and strode out of the stale shop and into the fresh air. "It seemed like a dream job," I sighed and cast a final look around, "but looks like it was just too good to be true."

"Leofe! Please, let me explain properly."

"No," I said and dug my keys out of my back pocket. "I think I've made a mistake. This place is amazing – *it was incredible, and I already loved it and felt instinctively that I belonged there* – but I don't think I'm quite what you're looking for."

"Oh, but you are, my dear."

"Don't let her leave!"

The horse whinnied then blew through its nose.

"The horse doesn't want me here!"

"We do! Please, don't go. We're sorry. This must all be so confusing."

"It is," I agreed.

"Then let us explain."

"Well ..."

"Please!"

Both Jodi and Aelfwen were giving me such pleading looks that I relented. "Sure, why not. What have I got to lose?"

"That's the spirit! Now, come back into the shop and Jodi will make us a cup of tea. Things are always better with a cup of tea."

"That's just what my mother always said."

"She did," Aelfwen agreed.

Minutes later, sitting in the shop's small kitchen as Jodi rinsed a small teapot then filled and plugged in an ancient kettle that looked as old as the Bakelite pre-war plug socket screwed to a block of wood loosely attached to the wall, Aelfwen cleared her throat and began to speak.

"So, Leofe, without wanting to upset you, or bring back difficult memories, you must have noticed how the animals react to you."

I nodded. "I guess."

"This was not always the case."

Again, I nodded.

"It started quite recently," she stated, "perhaps around the time of a great emotional upset?"

"Well ... yes. I've had a few ups and downs recently."

"I'd say!" Jodi said above the noise of the heating water.

"A little sympathy please, Jodi."

Did they know about Gerald? How could they? They couldn't. But then again, it had been in the newspaper, and the malicious rag had even published a desperately unflattering photograph of me and another, less unflattering, one of Cordelia, Gerald, and their children. The way it was worded made it sound as though they were the victims. Those had been dark days, some of my darkest, and thinking back, that *was* when Sir Galahad had begun to stay away from home. There were a number of other incidents too – another horse that had whinnied, reared up and fled across a field. I'd become used to the designer dogs that yapped as I walked past, barely noticing the increase in whining, and there had been a couple of cats that had crossed my path, hissed, arched their backs, then shot across the road to get out of my way. It all added up to being bizarre but damning evidence.

"You see, I am right," said Aelfwen with a pitying smile.

Had I spoken my thoughts aloud?

The kettle boiled and Leofe unplugged it then poured water into a waiting teapot.

"Yes, I suppose you are," I agreed, losing myself in thought as I watched the steam rise and mist the windowpanes making hazy the garden beyond. Painful memories flashed in my mind; the images as clear as though they were photographs. "Life's been kind of tough recently and," I said with self-pity beginning to poke, "there have been a few incidents with animals. They seem scared, I guess," I admitted.

Jodi nodded. "It's a natural reaction. Animals are intuitive. To them, you stink."

"Thanks!"

"It's the emotional toxins within you, dear. They are rather off-putting. Beatrice did mention them, but I have to say I'm quite surprised at how pungent the result is."

"So, I really do ... stink?" I took a sniff of my wrist. All I could smell was the – now obviously fake – perfume Gerald have given me last Christmas.

"Well ... the thing is not to worry, we're here in time."

"In time for what?" I asked although, with a sense of hope-lessness growing, I had no real interest in the answer.

"A detox."

"Exactly."

"A detox? How does that work? I'm not keen on starving myself and drinking gallons of green tea if that's what you're thinking."

Jodi shook her head. "See it as an intervention—like they do with alcoholics and drug addicts."

"I'm not an alcoholic! I had that blip but that was after my mother passed."

"No, of course you're not," Aelfwen soothed, "but you are addicted-"

"I am not an addict!" Chair legs scraped as I rose to leave.

Aelfwen flapped a hand, gesturing for me to sit back down. "Addicted to being miserable."

"I am not! I came here filled with hope. It was supposed to be a new adventure, but all I'm getting is the same old abuse!"

"Please, Leofe, sit down. I didn't mean to upset you."

"Don't let her upset you," Jodi said with a meaningful look at Aelfwen. "She hasn't got her social filter on!"

"Social filter? So much newfangled speech. I have no idea what you are saying half the time, Jodi. Now, Leofe, please let me explain and allow me to finish before you react. And you mustn't be despairing, that will only make things worse. The problem is that you've had years of abuse, so many of us do – people sense that we're dangerous to them and they try to destroy our power by subverting our ego-"

"Hark at you, Mrs Freud!"

Aelfwen shook her head. "Jodi, will you let me speak. So, the problem is that because of ill-treatment over the years, and particularly in the last five when your husband's betrayal ate at your core, the energy within you has become rotten. Magick needs an outlet and you've suppressed yours."

"I didn't know that Gerald had betrayed me until about six months ago."

"You knew, at a subconscious level, you knew. We witches always know. We sense betrayal like a thickly viscous trail of slime."

"Eww! Sounds gross," Jodi said.

"It is, dear. Sometimes it is so strong you can almost touch it."

"So, who will do it?" Jodi asked with an expectant smile. "The exorcism of this viscous slime?" She seemed to be enjoying my discomfort.

"Exorcism?" I began to grow concerned.

"Oh, Jodi. You're scaring the girl. Ignore her. She's a mischievous creature but you will learn how to deal with her—over time."

Jodi pulled a frown and her eyes glittered momentarily. Aelfwen wagged a finger. "You've been warned. Swige þú, wuduielfen."

"Sarigan, hlæfdige."

Aelfwen gave an accepting nod then returned her attention to me. "It's not an exorcism but we do need to rid you of all the emotional toxins that have built up within you. We need to give you a deep clean."

"You make me sound like an old carpet."

Jodi laughed.

"So, is that acceptable to you, Leofe?" Aelfwen asked.

"Can we burst that boil of festering poison?"

"Jodi!"

"Have you seen those videos where they lance boils, and the puss spurts out?"

"Oh, Jodi. Do stop."

"You're not lancing anything!" I said suddenly concerned that some hideous medical procedure was going to be performed.

"Don't worry, dear, Jodi is both mischievous and theatrical. It's more of a healing ceremony than a surgical removal of flesh."

"More of?"

"They suck out the poison then carve out the rotten flesh."

"What! I don't have any rotten flesh."

"On the videos, silly."

"Jodi do be quiet! You're making my stomach churn."

Mine was churning too. "I'm not doing anything until you've explained everything that happens. Exactly as it happens." *Why was I even agreeing? This was nuts!*

"Of course. Informed consent. You must know everything about the procedure, including any adverse events."

"Oh, Aelfwen, you do sound professional."

"Well, humans have gone astray so many times, we cannot follow suit. All must be known about any preventive or curative intervention. It's all about our rights, we must always cling onto those rights—bodily autonomy and all that."

"Indeed. Our inviolable rights are what stops persecution against us."

"Humans," I stated.

"'Humans', dear?"

"You said that '*we* cannot follow suit'."

"That's correct."

"So ... you're not human?"

Both looked down at me, eyes sparkling.

"Why, no, dear. And neither are you."

Chapter Eight

As a young child, I knew that I was different. It wasn't just the mean taunts from the kids in the playground, the ones who pointed, the ones who deliberately tripped me, or even the ones who poked at me and called me a witch, no, I just felt it. I wasn't like them. Don't get me wrong, I did have friends, some really good friends that I'm still in contact with more years later than I care to count, but I was just different. And then there were the things that happened when I thought about them, or the things I'd dreamt about that came true. Most of them are buried in my memories, but a few are singed there, like Barry's scream as he fell off the ladder.

The first incident I remember happened when I was just eight years old. Justin, a boy in my class, took an especial interest in tormenting me and would often make a beeline for me when we played tig. I still remember the way he'd punch at my arm and shout 'Tig!' then bowl into me or somehow manage to trip me up. Mum said that she thought he liked me—that's what boys did if they liked a girl, that or pull at their pigtails. I had pigtails too but was pretty sure that he was nasty just because ... well, looking back, he sensed I was different, an outsider, someone to be wary of. It's a human instinct, I guess, an 'othering' that has led to the deaths of thousands of witches and millions of humans over the centuries—a genocidal imperative. Anyway, one particular incident with the boy stuck in my mind.

Justin found a dead mouse.

Its eyes were glazed, and it had that thinness of body and dullness of fur that animals get once they've been dead a few days, but Justin picked it up and taunted us with it in the playground. The girls screamed then ran off giggling in horrified delight. I did too, until I noticed a wicked gleam in Justin's eyes as they met mine. He cornered me, held the mouse close, then pushed it into my face.

The mouse's nose and teeth brushed my lips.

My screams of revulsion only spurred him on, and he tried to force it into my mouth. The other kids stood around watching, some of the others even goading him on.

'Do it, Justin!' Patsy Jenkins shouted. 'Do it! Do it!'

The other kids joined in the chant until their voices drowned out my screams.

'Do it! Do it! Do it!'

He did it.

And the rancid taste of rotting mouse and the sensation of its fur clings to my memories.

I heaved, spitting out the mouse as unknown words filled my head. *Deád musincel þu bebítest se onæpling*

Justin stood in awe of what he had done and then burst into a cackling laugh, pointing at the dead mouse on the floor.

þu bebítest se onæpling

'I hate you!' I'd screamed. I didn't recognize the language the words flowed in, but I knew their meaning. 'It should bite you! I wish it would bite your tongue!'

Deád musincel þu bebítest se onæpling

I retched again, the stench of rotting mouse nauseating, and spat out more hairs. The crowd of jeering children had begun to fade away, some running as soon as they realized Justin had gone too far.

"She ate the mouse," Justin squawked in delight. "She ate a dead mouse!"

The mouse twitched.

Bent double with a now aching belly, I watched in curiosity then growing horror as the mouse continued to twitch then pulled itself onto all fours. Unsteady on tiny legs it tottered. The eyes remained glazed, the fur matted with spittle, its corpse emaciated, but it wobbled forward then scurried towards Justin.

"It's alive!" a girl in the audience screamed.

In the next moment, Justin's cackle morphed into a terrified scream as the zombie mouse crawled up his trousers then scrambled to his shoulder. His scream became panicked then hysterical as it jumped from his shoulder and onto his lips, its needle-like claws digging into his flesh. Justin's hysterical scream was no deterrent and it crawled into his mouth and bit down hard.

"She did it!" another girl shouted. "Leofe told the mouse to bite him!"

'She's a freak!'

'She's a witch!'

"Witch! Witch! Witch!"

What happened next is missing from my memory, but I may have been asked to stay off school for a few days or that may have been the incident that triggered a change in school. I can't say for sure; it's all a blur.

"So, Leofe, let's focus on the present."

Aelfwen's words broke through my daze and brought me back to the shop. Two pairs of sparkling eyes, one vivid green, the other a deep violet, looked down at me with concern.

"It's like glitter," I said. "My mum ... sometimes her eyes seemed to sparkle."

"Is she alright?"

"Yes, I think so, she just had ... a moment. Sensory overload. Some very interesting memories though; children can be so cruel."

"What about another cup of tea?" suggested Jodi. "That might help."

"Indeed, and I'll add a little something extra this time ... to help calm the nerves."

Jodi refilled the kettle and flipped the switch. The element began to hiss.

Aelfwen placed her hand over mine. "Leofe, are you alright?"

I managed to nod despite the feeling of being dazed. "Yes, I think I'm a bit tired, that's all."

"Indeed, you've had a long journey, and quite a surprise. It's an emotional time in any witch's life."

"I'm not a witch!" I protested, my ears still ringing with the memories of 'Witch! Witch! Witch!' being chanted in the playground.

"Oh, Leofe, you know that you are. You must have suspected it."

I twisted the ring my mother had worn her entire life. Aelfwen held out her hand and splayed her fingers on the table. She wore an identical ring.

"We're sisters, Leofe. You, me, Beatrice, your mother."

"You knew her?"

Aelfwen nodded. "We're all part of the same whole, a sisterhood of witches."

"A coven?"

"Yes, that's often a name given to a collection of witches." Her laugh was soft, subdued. "Some of us prefer a more solitary life, like your mother, and myself, whilst others like to live among their own."

"She died alone. No one came to the funeral. I buried her, alone."

Aelfwen's hand tightened around mine. "I know you buried her alone, but she didn't die alone. She had a good end, Leofe."

"And you know that how?"

"Well, I read the report."

My head throbbed.

"Your mother was very special ... to us all."

Jodi nodded her agreement. "She had a great sense of humour."

"She did. Gerald said she was weird, and that I was weird like her, but she wasn't weird at all, she was just my mum."

"Gerald was an ass!"

"Jodi! Language."

"He was a þeódloga. You can't deny it."

"No, you're right. He certainly often told lies." Aelfwen turned to me. "Your mother knew what Gerald was. She sensed his deceitfulness but knew that you had to discover that for yourself. It hurt her greatly to see you suffer. She would be glad to know that you are free of him now."

"Oh, I am."

"You are ... to an extent, and we will rid you of the last traces of anger that you hold towards him. Holding onto that anger keeps you tied to him, and that tether allows him to control you."

"How can he control me? He's not here. He doesn't call. I have no contact with him."

"No, but you're curdling from within because of your emotions, you are perpetually churning with anger. You must let go of him, Leofe, and then all the anger and poison will flow from you. You'll be new and fresh and ready for this next, wondrous part of your life."

"And who knows, maybe you'll find love again." Jodi's eyes sparkled. Aelfwen threw her a frown.

"No way! I've had enough of men to last me a lifetime. I'd rather be single."

"Sure," Jodie replied with a small laugh of amusement. "I'm not sure that's-"

"Swige þú, wuduielfen."

Jodi huffed in response, but her amused smile remained.

"I know this is all too much to take in at the moment," Aelfwen continued, "but it will become clear. We'll explain everything over the coming days, but let's focus on now. The detox. We're going to have to get on with it."

I mulled her words over.

Jodi placed another cup of tea in front of me. Aelfwen took a small porcelain bottle from her pocket and unscrewed the silver lid and let three drops of amber liquid drop into the cup.

"There, now drink that up and you'll feel a whole lot better and once we've taken you through the detox, you'll be your old self again."

"To be honest, I don't really want to be my old self again. I wasn't happy."

Aelfwen gave a sympathetic sigh. "I know, but I promise you this, your time at Blackwood Hall will be the beginning of a marvellous adventure."

"So, is she going to stay?" Jodi turned her attention to me.

Aelfwen held my gaze. "Are you?"

"Well, I promised myself that life would be an adventure and Blackwood Hall is certainly ... different." *And I already love it here!*

"Good, that's settled then. We can sign the contract later, but first-"

"I know, the detox."

"Exactly."

"You're right. About everything. Let's do it. Let's do this detox."

Outside, the whinnying of a horse was followed by the clamour of voices.

"Thor's hammer! What is going on?"

Chapter Nine

As suggested, I hung back as Aelfwen and Jodi disappeared through the door but quickly followed, curious to see exactly what was causing the commotion, and caught sight of a large woman marching out of the courtyard and two men striding forward with purpose. Out of hearing they drew into a close group. Aelfwen appeared to give instructions and the men left the courtyard along with Jodi. I withdrew into the shop as Aelfwen turned and waited.

Despite the men's obvious urgency, she appeared unflustered. "Ah, Leofe, we will have to postpone our little ceremony. Something has come up which I must take care of." She stood silent for a moment as though deep in thought. A frown appeared on her forehead but quickly disappeared. "Yes, that's what we'll do. Good. So, I will show you to your apartment. Come along."

Without further explanation, she turned and began to walk away with surprisingly quick and agile steps, and I had to pick up my pace to keep up with her.

"Do you have any luggage?"

"Yes, a bag. It's still on the bike."

"So, you packed light. Very good. I have a horrible habit of packing far too much. You will have to give me some tips."

"Well, there's not much I can carry on a bike so-"

"Very true. Well, there's no time to collect it now, but once I've shown you the apartment you can collect it at your leisure."

"Sure."

Suddenly businesslike and obviously distracted, I was curious to know what had happened to cause such a stir in the courtyard and change in her mood.

"Ignorance is bliss, sometimes, my dear," she murmured as we continued to walk apace. "Once you've settled ... then we'll introduce you to the others."

"I'd like that. Thanks."

"Well, it's a necessity, but be warned, some are rather ... eccentric."

We passed through the courtyard gate and stepped into the gardens at the rear of the house.

"Wow!"

The rear of the house with its extensive gardens was stunning. Formal gardens sprawled for a least an acre behind the house with the Courtyard being just one 'room' in it. They would take weeks to become familiar with, if not months. The area immediate to the back of the house was set to hard standing and laid with large stone slabs. Several ironwork patio tables painted white were set in front of a series of large French doors complete with matching chairs. It was the perfect space to sit and have breakfast on a summer morning. The two terraces beneath were set to grass but had wide borders filled with roses and peonies edged with clipped box hedging now in need of clipping. Rose covered arches, and arbours entwined with honeysuckle, added height. In summer the whole area would be rich with colour and filled with the heady scent of flowers in bloom.

As we reached the middle terrace, I noticed a secretive-looking pathway leading to another 'room' on my right, a secret garden. Flanked either side by a thick and towering hedge of privet the brickwork pathway, set in a classic herringbone pattern, led to an elaborate ironwork gate barely visible. A sign, too far away to read, was nestled within the hedge.

Despite Aelfwen's determination to get to the house at almost breakneck speed, I had to ask. "What's in there?"

"Behind the gate?" she asked without turning her head or breaking her stride.

"Yes."

"That's the Poison Garden."

"Looks intriguing."

"It's very special and needs a very special gardener to tend to it." She stopped and turned to me. "And that's why we've chosen you, Leofe."

I remembered the wilted plants at the nursery.

"Never mind that. Once you've been detoxified, all will be well."

We entered the house through a panelled door hung with massive iron hinges and opened with a circular ring of twisted iron.

"Now," she said as she twisted the ring and lifted the latch, "let's get you to your new home."

I followed her inside and up a staircase to what I presumed were the servants' quarters but from the stairs we entered a wide hallway. She led me to a large and heavy door and, swinging it open said, "Here you are. Home." Light from a massive window spilled out into the hallway. "Forgive me, Leofe, I'll have to leave you here, but make yourself at home and feel free to look around the grounds. The keys to the apartment are on the kitchen table. I'll show you the rest of the house, apart from the private apartments, of course, and introduce you to the rest of the staff later."

Left alone, and with the door now closed, I stood for several moments in awe. When the advert had mentioned apartment, I had imagined a tiny studio flat, but this room was magnificent with a tall, mullioned sash window that looked out onto the gardens. It was easily as large as the whole footprint of the house I had shared with Gerald. Decorated in modern neutral shades, a whiff of fresh paint suggested that it had been newly painted. An oversized dark green velvet sofa sat before a large fireplace already laid. A large wicker basket filled with logs sat waiting to feed it. Either side of the fire was a large armchair, both so big I could easily curl up in them to read. Hung above the mantle of the black marble fireplace was an enormous mirror in an elaborate silver gilt frame. Either side sat silver sconces complete with candles. I sighed, already imagining evenings in front of the fire sipping coffee and reading a favourite novel.

"This is heaven!" I whispered as I stepped further into the room, noticing the chandelier that hung from the ceiling. "Beautiful!" I sighed. "Definitely not the servants' quarters."

Huge doors either side of the chimney breast remained closed. I decided to open the one closest to the inner wall of the apartment.

It led to the bedroom. "Wow!" I laughed with excitement. Again, I was faced with a stunning room. Painted a soft and chalky white with a single wall papered in a chinoiserie style paper, a huge rug covered much of the floor, leaving dark and wide floorboards to show at the edges. A wide mahogany dressing table, complete with stool and triple mirror sat between the windows, but a four-poster bed complete with embroidered drapes to match the wallpaper was the showstopper. Plump pillows encased in white cotton peaked out from beneath a matching duvet. Despite the dark furniture, the room was light with no hint of the mustiness that had overpowered the shop in the courtyard. A door at the far side of the room led to a bathroom twice the size of the one back at home. Wooden panels painted in the same chalky white extended to shoulder height. Above them, the walls were papered in another chinoiserie paper. A huge mirror sat above a large vanity unit within which sat a rectangular sink and behind it on the opposite wall was a glass-encased shower. Like the living room, and bedroom, the bathroom was immaculate.

The door on the other side of the fireplace led to a small galley-style kitchen in painted wood with solid wooden counter tops. The appliances appeared unused. In fact, it all appeared to be newly installed and of far better quality than I had ever had at home. An archway led to a panelled dining area again painted chalky white. At its centre was a circular pine table with four ladder-back chairs. A sash window looked out over the gardens.

I walked from room to room in disbelief. Yesterday I had despaired of finding a decent place to live – the flats and houses I'd viewed within my price range had been small, damp, or just unpleasant. "Amazing!" I repeated. "This is just ... incredible."

The cupboards were stocked with essentials: bread, butter, marmalade, bacon, eggs, mushrooms, and even black pudding—everything I enjoyed for breakfast. And there were my favourite brands of tea and coffee too. I decided to make myself a cup of tea and sat on the sofa staring at the unlit fire with the sun streaming in from the almost floor to ceiling windows revelling in the beauty of the apartment soaking up moments of pure happiness.

With the tea drunk, I collected my bags from the bike and returned to the apartment. It took all of five minutes to place my belongings in the chest of drawers. The only item of real value I had brought with me was my mother's herbal and I placed that on the table in the living room and then sat back down on the sofa unsure what to do next. Despite the beauty of my surroundings, it was impossible to relax. Yesterday I was miserable and practically destitute, now I had a new job and a new home, and not just any new job or home, a completely amazing, dream-fulfilling job and home. "It's just beautiful," I repeated to myself. "It's too good to be true!" At that moment a chink of doubt set in, and a wave of anxiety washed over me. It *was* too good to be true and it would all come crashing down at any minute! Unable to settle, I walked to the window, and scanned the gardens. Beyond the formal clipped hedges and pathways that separated the 'rooms' of the larger gardens lay the secretive pathway that led to the poison garden. Bounded by tall hedges the flower beds in the garden were laid out in triangular patterns that I realized created a pentagram. A wooden 'house' with a steep and turfed roof sat to one corner. A trail of smoke plumed from its chimney. I badly wanted to see inside the house; it had to be more than a tool shed.

With the afternoon drawing to a close, I decided to make the most of the last rays of sunshine and take the bike out onto the winding lanes. Riding free always soothed me and, in my increasingly anxious state – afraid that this joyful experience wouldn't last – I needed to lose myself on the road.

Chapter Ten

The sun burned a dark orange as I kick-started the engine into life. Gerald had laughed at my choice of bike, a vintage Norton Commando Roadster, preferring a more modern BMW and buying all the modern conveniences, bragging to his mates about how much the latest sat nav, top box, exhaust etcetera had cost him. My bike, although in perfect working order, was no match for the speed and accelerating power that his bike had. In the early days, we'd love the go out riding together, but it had soon become a chore as he always had to be in the lead and we always had to go to the destination he picked, following the route he had plotted out. I gave up biking for many years as going out with him sucked all the joy from the experience, but when he began staying away from home for longer and longer periods, including the weekends, and our holidays from work never coincided, I started biking again.

Wednesdays were Bike Night in our county, and I'd team up with a few friends and we'd visit the pub that was that night's destination. Biking was dominated by men, but I'd never had a problem with that. Most of them were friendly and I guess I never gave off 'I'm available' vibes. They knew I was happily married, at least that was my cover story. It was the married biker couples that caused me grief. Some of the wives rode pillion and a fair few had their own bikes, but their happiness always tweaked my pain and made me feel lonely.

The engine growled as I rode through the narrow lanes, leaning into the bends. Dappled light shone through the overhanging canopy, growing dark where the leaves were thickening as Spring grew to Summer.

Blackwood Hall was nestled in a valley, and I climbed the hills passing through woodlands and then past open fields dotted with sheep. After several miles, I passed through a village that was not much more than a group of houses along the road with a single shop and a stone church set back on a hill.

Earlier tension eased from my shoulders and with it any grating thoughts of Gerald and his betrayal, or anxiety about Blackwood Manor and my new job. The road was my focus, and the trees, ferns, fields, drystone walls, and the setting sun, medicine for my soul. Relieved and feeling refreshed, I turned the bike around and began my journey back to Blackwood Hall, cleansed of all negative energies and thoughts—biking was my own personal detox.

What Aelfwen meant by a detox was still a mystery but if it involved any kind of weird rituals, or starving myself, then there was no way I was going to participate in it—the animals would just have to get used to me.

Journeying back along the roads, with the sun falling to twilight and the dappled light growing weaker, the overhung roads became tunnels. I recognized the road and expected the turn off for Blackwood Hall to appear around one of the oncoming bends.

In a split second, as I rounded yet another bend in the tunnel of overhanging trees, the illusion of inner peace was shattered as a massive form threw itself at me from the gloom. Instinct took over and I twisted the handlebars, forcing the bike to the side of the road. A horse reared and I was dwarfed by more than one thousand pounds of muscular stallion, its hooves poised directly above me just as I was headed for the solid drystone wall that edged the narrow lane.

Hooves slammed into the ground, narrowly missing me as I grappled with the handlebars, desperate to avoid the wall, but although the front tyre missed, the foot peg caught against the stone, and I lost control. The bike spun, the impact throwing me off, and I landed with a thud on my back, my helmet hitting the road. I bounced again then rolled to a stop. Radiating throughout my body, the pain was intense, and I lay in stunned paralysis. The bike's engine cut out and, as it silenced, I heard a man's pained grunts mingled with the horse's nickering snorts.

I lay dazed, pain surging, obliterating thought.

Unable to move, I tried to make sense of where I was and what had happened. The events are clearer now, but in that moment, I lay in a fog of bewilderment. Time passed as I lay recovering from the shock until my senses returned enough for me to check over my body. Slowly I began to move my limbs, checking hands, legs, and arms for lack of movement. The pain was acute and throbbing, but not agonizing, and each of my limbs moved, so I doubted any broken bones. I had landed on my back without trauma to my stomach and the helmet had absorbed the impact of my head hitting the road. There would be bruises, but I seemed to have escaped without real injury. I rolled over onto my front, slowly pushed up onto all fours, then staggered to a stand. Pain ripped down my leg. The horse snorted, whinnied, then reared. A man groaned

The bike lay strewn across the lane, back wheel spinning as the agitated horse stepped backwards and forwards. The fallen man lay against the opposite wall, his face to the stonework.

He groaned again and rolled onto his back. Although the light was failing, I could see that he was a large man, at least six foot tall with broad shoulders, casually dressed in jeans and a plaid shirt beneath a dark gilet. There was no sign of a riding helmet which meant he could have sustained serious head injuries.

"Are you alright?" It was a stupid question, of course he wasn't alright.

He grunted a reply. I took a step forward. The horse whinnied and snorted, eyeing me with suspicion.

"There now," I soothed. "There now, no need to be afraid." Despite the horse, I had to help the man. "Can you move?" I asked, unsure whether I could get past the horse safely. The man grunted, then pushed himself to a sitting position and sat with head in hands. No broken bones—please!

"No thanks to you," he muttered, his voice gruff.

I was taken aback. How could I be the one in the wrong? He was the one galloping in the middle of the road. He groaned again.

"Can I help? Are you hurt?"

He batted his hand at me as though swatting a fly. Liquid gleamed at his temple. I took another tentative step closer. He was bleeding.

"I think you're hurt," I said.

"No kidding!"

Ignoring his rudeness, I limped to my bike. I wasn't the most organized person in the world, but I always carried a small first aid kit with me. I retrieved the torch from my panniers along with the first aid pouch—a bandage, some plasters, cotton swabs, and disinfecting wipes. I hobbled back, the pain in my left leg wasn't getting any easier to bear.

Torchlight shone in the lowering twilight, pushing back the growing shadows and illuminated the man. Behind me the horse whinnied its distrust, and I made each movement calm so that I didn't spook it further. He squinted into the light, shielding his eyes with hands that matched his large frame. Torchlight picked out a strong jaw, speckled with dark stubble and full lips.

"Sorry!" I moved the light. "It looks like you're bleeding. Can I take a look?"

"I'm fine," he grunted and attempted to stand but quickly gave up.

"Let me help."

"I'll be fine in a minute. I don't need your help."

"Oh."

With a grunt, he grabbed the wall and pulled himself up to a stand. "What the devil do you think you were doing?"

"Me?"

"Yes, you. You could have killed us."

"You could have killed me!"

"You were riding in the middle of the road."

I wasn't going to take this. He was the one who had appeared out of nowhere and caused me to crash. "You were galloping in the middle of the road."

"You should have had your lights on, then you would have seen me."

The comment stung; the light had been failing. "Well, even so, I don't have x-ray vision. I wouldn't have seen you."

"No, but I would have seen you."

"You must have heard me? The bike's not silent."

He grunted. We were at an impasse, neither willing to admit that we were wrong. The evening continued to grow darker.

The horse snorted and pawed at the ground. He walked across to it and took the reins before patting its flanks. "Steady on, boy. Steady on," he soothed. The horse snorted and rubbed the side of its long snout against his arm. "There now. There now."

"Is your horse alright?"

"He would appear to be, no thanks to you. You could have killed us."

"Hey! I got hurt too and my bike looks like it's in worse shape than your horse."

He grunted. I gritted my teeth. He was stubborn.

"Listen, neither of us are hurt. Let me help you lift your bike."

Was he relenting? "You should get that cut checked out," I said shining the light at his temple. Blood had trickled into his sideburn and was smeared across his temple. "Looks like it may need stitches."

"I'll be fine," he repeated.

"Can I at least take a look?" I asked holding up my first aid kit. "I've done a first aid course at work. I could help. Clean it up for you?"

"No," he replied, "but ... thanks for the offer."

Another stalemate.

"Fine," I replied. "At least I tried. You should get checked out at the hospital though. Shall we swap insurance details?"

"Huh? No. You're alive. I'm alive. My horse is alive. I say we leave it at that."

"But ... my bike. It will need repairing."

Once again, he grunted, but this time with pain as he reached inside his back pocket and pulled out his wallet. "Here." He thrust a wad of notes towards me. "This will cover it."

"But it's-"

"Listen, we're both alive despite your best efforts to kill me-"

"That's not fair."

"We're both alive," he repeated. "No real harm done. Let's leave it at that."

Still shaken, adrenaline now coursing through my body, I realized that no amount of talking would change this man's mind. There was something stonelike in his determination.

He thrust the wad at me once more. "Take the money, or don't take the money, but this ends here."

I reached for the money and bit back my automatic response of 'thanks'. "Right."

"Right. Well, good."

He stroked the horse's mane, then with another grunt of pain, slipped a boot through the stirrup and hauled himself into the saddle. "From now on, be more careful on these roads; there's worse here than me to run into."

With a tug at the reins, he urged the horse on, and I watched in silence as he disappeared within the darkness of the lanes.

Chapter Eleven

A quick check of the motorbike showed the damage to be superficial scratches to the tank's paintwork and a scuffed exhaust. That was galling, but the money the man had given me in compensation would just about cover it and I wasn't the vindictive type so not interested in seeking 'damages' for 'emotional distress'!

"Men!" I muttered as I kickstarted the bike. It hummed into life with no evidence of damage to the engine. I checked for any other damage, particularly to the brake and oil pipes before setting off. Night had almost fallen as I arrived back at the Hall, and I parked my bike and hobbled my way back to the apartment.

I met no one on the way across the grounds or as I went up the stairs and stood in front of the apartment's door still disbelieving that this really was my new home. The door swung open and once again breath caught in my chest. The curtains had been drawn and the fire lit. Either side of the mirror, candles flickered, their light reflected in the silver wall sconces. The effect was beautiful, and I felt even more as though I were stepping into a dream.

In the kitchen I filled the kettle and then noticed the table in the dining area where a bottle of wine sat beside a silver dome with a white envelope propped against it. On the front was written 'Leofe'. I unfolded the note inside. Written in a beautiful calligraphic script was, 'Welcome to Blackwood Hall!' and it was signed 'All the staff'. The bottle was a Rioja Reserva and beneath the silver dome was a bowl of beef stew with dumplings. A note at the side gave heating instructions. My belly growled its hunger.

An hour later, a glass of wine in hand, the beef stew eaten, I sat in front of the fire, cossetted by the velvet sofa, mulling over the day, floating close to joy. Life, over the course of twenty-four hours, had become surreal, and I was struggling to believe that I wasn't in a dream and that at any moment I'd wake up to discover myself in bed at the B&B or worse, at my old home, on the inflatable camping bed I'd kept out of storage so that my last night at the house wasn't too uncomfortable. I gave the skin on the back of my wrist a gentle pinch. It felt real. I took another small sip of wine, determined to make it last and not get tipsy on my first night. Memories of the accident kept intruding, but I pushed them away. Afterall, as the man had said, we were both alive and no real damage had been done. His attitude had irked me, but we could all overreact when startled, and being thrown off your horse would do that to a person. I'd had worse days. Worse accidents. Worse men to deal with. I took another sip of wine, sighed, and enjoyed the feeling of warmth emanating from the fire. Life! It threw rocks at you one day, and offered you roses and chocolates the next.

Outside an owl hooted and somewhere in the distance, perhaps among the woodlands, a fox barked. Fire crackled in the hearth. I took another sip of wine and relaxed another fraction, allowing my eyes to close. Sleep beckoned.

Memories floated as I slipped into semi-consciousness and I relived the scene in the lane in a dream-like, fearless state. Each second of the accident drew out as though filmed in slow motion. The horse's hooves were above me. This time I saw the rider on its back and, as the horse reared, he pulled at the reins, forcing the horse higher and to the side—saving me from being stamped beneath the muscular stallion.

In that moment, our eyes met.

His were a brilliant topaz with an outer iris of dark caramel. For what seemed like seconds but could only have been milliseconds - if it had even really happened - he held my gaze and captured me there. And then he smiled. And I was hit by a wave of desire.

A knock at the door jolted me out of my sleep. Red wine sloshed up the side of the glass, the wave peaking at its lip, then washed back down without spilling.

"Stupid dream!"

Relieved that the wine hadn't spilled over the carpet or sofa but perturbed by the emotion my reimagining of the accident had aroused, I answered the door.

"Good evening, Leofe. I hope you don't mind the intrusion." Aelfwen stood in the doorway, immaculate and petite, her delicate features perfectly framed by pure white pixie-cut cropped hair. Green eyes held mine and I noticed a flash of concern and how dark around the iris her eyes had become. There was no evidence of the sparkle I had seen earlier in the day.

"No, not at all," I answered and opened the door further. "Please, come in."

"I see you've settled in already," she smiled and gestured to the wine glass on the coffee table and the fire in the hearth.

There was no hint of accusation in her voice. Gerald would have pointed to the glass and made some insinuation about me drinking 'again'.

"Can I get you a glass?"

"That would be lovely, Leofe. Yes, thank you."

I fetched another glass from the kitchen then poured generously. She took the drink with a smile. "This is one of my favourites," she confided. "I thought that you'd like it."

"I do, thank you."

We sat together on the sofa. Aelfwen seemed happy to sit in silence and sip her wine before the fire. "This has always been one of my favourite rooms in the house."

"It's gorgeous. I just can't believe that it's where I get to live. Are you sure I'm supposed to be here? I mean—it's so grand, and I'm just the gardener."

"Oh, you're so much more than just the gardener, Leofe. You're the Head Gardener and well, there are some tasks that will require something a little more than the usual trimming of hedges etcetera."

"Tasks?"

"Yes. The Poison Garden, for example, you'll have a special role to play there."

"Does it attract many visitors?" I asked, remembering my visit to the poison garden at Alnwick, one of the stately home's biggest draws.

"Well, you could say that, although ... Anyway, I digress." She took another sip of wine. "I came here to collect you, not talk about your duties, we can do that during working hours. Jodi is waiting."

"Collect me?"

"Yes, dear. The detox. Remember?"

Inwardly, I groaned. "I'm feeling much better to be honest. I went out on my bike earlier—I find that therapeutic ..." I offered.

"That's lovely, dear." She placed her glass on the coffee table.

"So ... perhaps I don't need a detox?"

She rolled her eyes. "Now, now. There's nothing to worry about. Don't take notice of Jodi going on about festering pustules and the like. She wasn't being literal—it's just an analogy. And no, we won't be forcing gallons of green tea down you either."

"Then what?"

"Oh, you'll see. Now, come along. We really must get that negative energy out of you. Tomorrow is a big day."

"Right." I was unconvinced.

Aelfwen ignored my reticence and stood in the doorway. "Come along, Leofe. It's time."

Her green eyes sparkled.

Go with her, Leofe.

The resistance I felt slipped away and was replaced with an urge to follow.

Chapter Twelve

Globes hovered impossibly above the still waters; their light diffused by a mist that covered its banks. I stood at the water's edge, naked except for a light cotton shift that Aelfwen had exchanged for my clothes. Despite the low hanging fog, the stars twinkled in a cloudless midnight blue sky with the moon huge and brilliant above. The night air was chill.

"Step in," Aelfwen urged.

"But it's cold," I complained.

"The sooner you do it, the sooner it will be over."

"But surely ... Isn't there another way to detox?"

"Well, there is, but you wouldn't like it. Far more dangerous."

"This is going to be dangerous?"

"No, the other method is far more dangerous."

"Far more—so there is an element of danger in this?"

"No, not really. It's just cold."

I dipped a toe into the water. "You're not kidding. It's freezing."

"Yes, and I am getting cold stood here. Let's to it."

From the woodlands came the chitter of an unseen creature. An owl hooted. A fox cried, its call an eerie and wailing scream.

"Listen to them, they're getting excited too."

The night did seem to be filled with sound once you grew quiet and listened. I took a step into the water and then another until the shift floated then grew heavy.

"Go into the middle. Let the water caress you."

Despite nagging doubts, and disbelief that I had allowed Aelfwen to convince me to strip off beside the pond then wade into freezing water with goodness knows what beneath, I felt compelled to obey and walked steadily into the middle. The globes hovering above grew in brightness as I approached the centre and then dimmed to cast a soft and diffused glow around me. The edges of the pond disappeared along with Aelfwen on the bank, and I was alone shrouded by mist. A sense of peace enveloped me and when voices began to chant and then figures emerged from the haze, I accepted it without question or concern. Voices sang, low and melodic in a language I didn't understand. The mist grew to a brilliant white as a circle of naked women stepped closer, tightening the circle around me. Beneath me the water grew deep, and the weight of the cloth pulled me down. There was no sense of fear and the light that illuminated the air above illuminated the depths of the water. The women swam now, gliding through the water as though mermaids, swirling faster and faster until they became a blur. Deep within me emotion welled. Despair. Anxiety. Grief. The sensation was overwhelming and with it came tightness in my chest and a desperate need for breath. The weight of the shift, so diaphanous before I had stepped into the pond was now a lead weight, dragging me down. The women continued to swirl around me, their flaxen hair streaming. I yearned to sob, to howl the grief that was growing within me, to wallow in the sensation of self-pity. It grew, suffocating, robbing me of breath and just as I felt I would explode with the pressure, hands grabbed my arms, and I was thrust to the surface. My gasp of breath was followed by a low groan from the core of my being that filled the night.

Time was nothing to me and I stood completely unaware of my surroundings as waves of grief and a dark and painful wallowing energy left my body. Finally, everything grew silent, and I became aware of the cold tingling of my skin. Water lapped against my thighs and the cotton shift clung to my naked body. I shivered suddenly aware of a cold breeze brushing against my skin and opened my eyes to a clear, dark sky sprinkled with stars. The moon, huge and low, shone its light on the water. It lapped against my thighs with silvery waves.

The women were gone and the haze of sparkling light that had hidden the woodland had disappeared. Even Aelfwen was nowhere to be seen. I was alone.

Arms crossed over my front for warmth, I waded to the bank. Lights from the house shone in the distance but it was torchlight that caught my attention.

"Aelfwen!" I whispered. "Aelfwen!" She didn't respond and I stood on the bank. The clothes I had handed to Aelfwen were nowhere to be seen.

An owl hooted and twigs snapped.

"Aelfwen!" I called. Alone, with the elation now fading, I began to grow uneasy. I was alone, in the dark, and wet. It had been magical, an astonishing moment of awe, and I wanted to share my experience with Aelfwen, ask her if I was detoxified, if I was no longer 'poisonous'. Time passed and as there was no sign of Aelfwen, I decided to make my own way back to the house. The shift clung to my body, the fabric moulding to my breasts, belly, and thighs. Water trickled down my legs. I decided to take it off, wring it out, then make my way to the house, hopeful that by then Aelfwen would have returned, hopefully with my clothes and a towel.

As I pulled the wet cloth up and over my head, my naked-ness exposed, I heard the crunch of footsteps, followed by an exclamation.

"Oh!"

It was a man's voice!

Unable to disentangle the wet cloth to pull it back down and hide my nakedness, I desperately pulled at the fabric, yank-ing it over my head, then clutching it to my body.

To my relief, the man had turned his back, and was walking away. Nevertheless, I stepped back into the pond, and took a sidestep behind some reeds.

My heart hammered as my cheeks began to burn.

"Leofe!"

Aelfwen! "I'm here!" I whispered.

"Where? I can't see you."

"Are you alone?"

"No."

"Right," I muttered. There was no way I was going to step out into the open with him there. The only saving grace was that he probably hadn't seen my face – everything else perhaps – but not my face, so I was anonymous, unknown. If I stepped out, he'd know exactly who I was—whoever he was. No doubt he was one of the staff, a gardener perhaps given he was out late at night.

A giggle interrupted my train of thought, and I recognized the voice. "Who's with you—exactly?"

"Just Jodi. I forgot to bring a towel. I thought that you might want one."

"Might!"

Jodi giggled again.

"Why are you hiding?"

"There was a man."

"Oh, I see, well he's not here now and the staff here are used to seeing unusual things."

"I'm not used to being the unusual thing!" I quipped.

I stepped out from the reeds.

"You're naked!"

Jodi giggled.

I waded to the edge, the shift covering my front. "I was cold, the shift was dripping, and you were nowhere to be seen. I thought that if I wrung it out-"

"And did this man ... see you in the water?"

"Not exactly."

"Out of the water?"

"Yes."

"Like this?" she gestured to my disrobed state.

"Worse! I was taking the shift off over my head when I heard him. I don't know what he saw, but when I saw him, he was walking away."

"It was Maximus," Jodi stated. "I just passed him on the way back."

Aelfwen groaned.

"Who is Maximus?"

"That would be Maximus Blackwood."

"Blackwood? The owner?"

"Yes."

"My boss!"

"Yes."

"But he ... he's just seen me stark naked!"

Jodie giggled. "Oh, don't worry. You look good for your age."

"Jodi!"

"Well, she does. She has a lovely figure. Nice boobs, bum's not too saggy."

"Swige þú, wuduielfen."

Quiet wood elf. Although the words were unknown to me, my brain translated the words. I watched Jodi closely, noticing the mirthful smile and bright eyes, their violet irises sparkling in the moonlight. She did look elfish, in a *Lord of the Rings* kind of way.

"Jodi, why did Maximus come down here? It's not usual for him to do so."

Jodi remained silent but her eyes glittered as she fought against a smile.

"Did you tell him to come here?"

She shook her head. "No, I never would do that," she replied.

Her tone was totally unconvincing. "You told him to come down here?" I challenged.

"No."

She wasn't being truthful. Aelfwen had mentioned that she was mischievous, but this was beyond the pale. Why would she do that? Just for fun? To embarrass me? "I need to lay down," I said, suddenly weary. Jodi may find the situation amusing, but mortification was taking hold.

"Now, now. Don't get yourself in a tizzy over this, Leofe. Maximus has seen many ... unusual sights."

"Right."

"I mean to say, he's a man of ... a man of great ... erm, understanding."

Jodi chuckled. "I'm sure he liked what he saw."

"Jodi!"

I groaned. "It's so humiliating!"

"Now, don't fret, Leofe. He ... well, he probably won't even remember this tomorrow. He's a busy man."

"Thanks!"

"And it was dark," she offered.

"He had a torch," I recounted. "I was pulling off the shift. I was stood on the bank, naked."

Jodi snorted. "He got an eyeful then!"

"Oh ... well, you know what I mean though. Don't make a mountain out of a molehill." Aelfwen offered me a neatly folded pile of clothes.

My new boss catching me stark naked, beside a pond, at night, was not a molehill! I sighed and thanked Aelfwen for the clothes.

Chapter Thirteen

The door to my apartment closed with a soft thud and I sighed with relief as the craziness of the day was shut out. A warm orange glow illuminated the hearth and although the fire had burned low, the room remained warm. The ceremony may have washed out my 'toxic emotions' but I had pond weed in my hair and mud on my feet and I kept getting a whiff of a faint but definite sulphuric odour. I showered, washed my hair, soaped the smelly silt from between my toes, then sat before the fire drying my hair with the day playing back through my mind.

I remained mortified by what had happened at the pond and had even considered packing my bags and leaving. How could I face my boss after what he had seen? But if I left I'd lose everything, and everything here was perfect. Even with the burning sensation of shame on my cheeks as I remembered his surprise of 'Oh!' I felt joy at being sat in front of the fire in this beautiful room. And who knows, perhaps he wouldn't know it was me. Afterall, my face had been hidden by the wet shift. I poured myself a small glass of wine and sat mulling the day over as my hair dried.

The past days had been bizarre. The past days had been wonderful. And I had promised myself that life would be an adventure. And this, I realized, was the adventure! Despite my embarrassment, I decided that I would stay. Afterall, Jodi said that I looked good for my age so perhaps I shouldn't be quite so embarrassed.

Sleep beckoned and, exhausted, I slipped into bed and managed to fall to sleep despite the constant ebb and flow of memories. As I slipped into unconsciousness, I took with me an image of the dark-haired stranger from the lane. Broad-shouldered and muscular beneath a plaid shirt, the man sat astride the rearing stallion, his eyes locked to mine as I sat beneath its hooves. It was so clear I felt as though I could reach out to touch the massive creature. Trapped as though in a still from a film, I raised my arm and just as the stranger opened his mouth to speak, I woke to a screech.

Immediately alert, I sat up in bed, ready to jump out if the noise repeated. For several minutes I listened until, from somewhere in the gardens, a fox barked. There were other noises too—the creaking of joists and an odd knocking noise. I lay back down, relieved. The house, vast and old, was settling, as houses do as temperature cools during the night, and we were in a rural idyll surrounded by wildlife. There were bound to be noises I wasn't used to; it would just take a little time. I closed my eyes and readjusted my pillow, hoping that sleep would take me quickly but less than a minute passed before I heard the bang of a door followed by shouting. The voices were muffled, and I couldn't tell if they were men's or women's, or both. This time I remained still, listening carefully. The banging of a door repeated. It came from above.

I decided to investigate.

The next floor was the top floor and above that would be an attic. It was an old house and enormous house, and I knew that many had attics where servants would have had rooms or were boarded out and used for storage.

The flight of steps to the attic was narrow and steep. Every step I took seemed to make the wooden boards creak and I hovered at the return where the stairs continued to climb. At the top of that flight was a door. From beyond the door there came the sound of footsteps and low voices. Footsteps grew louder and then a door opened. Harsh laughter grew loud then quietened as the door opened and closed. It wasn't the laugh of someone sharing a joke, it was mocking and laced with anger and came from a woman. I retreated, turning to run down the stairs with a light step and walked quickly back down the corridor as someone exited the attic room and came down the stairs.

I withdrew along the corridor and waited. At the bottom of the stairs, a figure appeared. The light was low, and much of the hallway was still in shadow, but it looked like the heavy-set woman I had spotted scurrying across the courtyard when Aelfwen had been called away during our initial meeting. I retreated further into the shadows expecting the floorboards to creak and betray me, desperately searching for an excuse as to why I was lurking in the corridors at midnight but, to my relief, she took the opposite direction and disappeared into the shadows further along. A door opened and closed, and I made my way back to the apartment. Whatever was going on upstairs was probably a domestic issue and none of my business and I had no doubt that I would be introduced to the rest of the staff tomorrow—and the owner. I groaned at the thought. Tomorrow would be embarrassing!

Chapter Fourteen

The following morning, I woke to the sound of birdsong and grey light pushing at the edges of the drawn curtains. Dawn was breaking on my first day in my new job. Unlike yesterday, I wasn't late, and I luxuriated in minutes spent reflecting on how my life had changed, as though on the toss of a coin.

Today, was the beginning of a new life. Today was the day I would meet my new boss. Today was the day I would face the man who had seen me as a full-frontal nude!

Oh, hell!

"Just forget about it, Leofe!" I muttered. "Don't let it spoil things."

How can I forget it?

It's no big deal.

Sure, apart from the fact that the guy has seen my fifty-one-year-old body naked.

Hey! Don't be so harsh on yourself. Jodi said you have nice boobs, and your bum isn't too saggy.

So, that means it's a bit saggy!

Oh, shut up, Leofe!

The internal dialogue continued, but I made my best efforts to drown it out with thoughts about how wonderful my apartment was and focused on making breakfast.

After quickly washing up and downing my second cup of coffee, I made my way to the courtyard and was surprised to find it bustling with activity. As I entered two men appeared carrying boxes, obviously making a delivery. Jodi stood at the open door of one of the buildings. A man dressed in worn jeans, plaid shirt, and wellington boots pushed a wheelbarrow filled with horse manure whilst a young boy emerged from a stable, shovel in hand. As I took it all in and waved to Jodi, two riders on horseback appeared at the main entrance. One I recognized as the man from the lane, the other, to my surprise, was Aelfwen.

They made their way towards the stables and then dismounted. Aelfwen waved and gestured for me to approach.

"This is Leofe Swinson, Mr. Blackwood. She's to be our new Head Gardener."

Maximus Blackwood towered above me. Broad-shouldered, his muscular arms and chest obvious beneath his casual shirt, he dwarfed Aelfwen. With an amused smile already on his lips, the intensity of his gaze took me by surprise. Topaz eyes ringed with caramel took me in. The man exuded strength and a dangerous, barely contained, energy. "We've already met."

"Oh."

"She nearly killed me." His eyes met mine, and held them, his smile mirthful. "And, I think we may have had a second encounter."

The heat in my cheeks was instant; he recognized me from the pond!

"Do you often enjoy a swim at midnight, Mistress Swinson?"

He may be my boss, and good-looking, but I'd had a gut full of being mocked by Gerald and, in my new incarnation, in this new life, I wasn't prepared to take it anymore. I decided to brazen it out. "I do, Mr. Blackwood," I replied with my best effort at sounding sincere. "The cold water is so refreshing." I smiled. "Perhaps you'd like to join me one night?"

Aelfwen sucked in her breath. Jodi tittered.

A quizzical frown crossed his face. "Ah, well, yes," he said taken aback. He recovered quickly and returned my smile. "Well, you never know. I may just take you up on that offer."

He turned and patted the stallion's mane. A young boy appeared from the stable and took hold of the reins. Maximus glanced at me then turned to Aelfwen as the boy led the horse back inside. "Aelfwen, you have made an interesting choice."

She nodded. "I think so, but a good one."

"I hope so. Bring her to my office later—once you've shown her the grounds." Without waiting for a reply, Maximus Blackwood turned and began to walk away. "Walk with me, Aelfwen."

As Aelfwen walked obediently by his side, Jodi stepped to mine. "What do you think of our boss, Leofe? Do you like him?"

"He's arrogant!" I blurted. "Arrogant and conceited and full of himself."

"And gorgeous! He's gorgeous isn't he."

"I haven't noticed," I lied. "He's too old for you, though."

"Hah! Far too old. But not for you."

Despite her cheek, I liked this girl. "I'm not sure whether to be offended by that, Jodi."

She laughed. "But you do find him attractive, don't you," she stated.

"I haven't given it any thought."

"I bet you do, though. He's so handsome."

I laughed and shook my head. He certainly was an attractive man, but he was arrogant, and my boss. "Oh, Jodi. I've had enough of men to last me a lifetime."

Chapter Fifteen

As I waited for Aelfwen to return, I explored the shop. She had said that I was to be in charge, which was not a role I wanted, and I chatted to Jodi in the hope that she would be interested in taking a major part in running the place. To my relief, she had plenty of ideas of how she wanted to 'transform' the room, had already been checking out the competition, and made a list of alterations she thought would bring the shop into the 'modern world'.

"I love the brickwork," she said, "and the wooden beams are beautiful. I'd like to keep the look natural, so no plastic shelving."

"I agree. We need to enhance the character of the place rather than hide it."

"Exactly! I'm so glad that you think that way too. I've been doing some research," she said pulling out a mobile phone. "Look at this. Tell me what you think."

The screen showed what looked like a loft apartment. It was far larger than the shop, but the aesthetic was similar – bare bricks, and wooden beams – and I understood why Jodi thought the style would work here. There were open shelves made of rustic looking wood, very possibly renovated scaffolding boards, held onto the wall using chunky black iron brackets. The kitchen worktop was of natural wood whilst the cupboards were a mixture of painted black and reclaimed pine. There were plants everywhere and they looked particularly stunning beside the black painted furniture.

"What's great is that we've got most of the furniture and shelving here already. It just needs a bit of work and I've seen a massive Welsh dresser in one of the storage sheds that would look amazing painted black and stood against that wall." She pointed to the long expanse of wall behind me.

"It would," I agreed, already imaging it in place and stacked with plants, "but I'm not sure I'll have time for flipping furniture."

Her eyes gleamed. "I know, but I do, and I'd love to do it. I can't wait to tell Aelfwen. She's been talking about getting some modern kitchen cabinets in here just because it makes things easier. I've been putting her off."

"Modern furniture would spoil the atmosphere in here," I said. "The energy would be lopsided."

For a moment, Jodi examined me. "Aelfwen really did make a good choice," she smiled. "You understand it."

"Understand?"

"Yes. The energy, how it can so easily be tipped the wrong way."

"I was a walking advertisement for it yesterday," I said, "but the horse didn't complain when it saw me today."

Jodi nodded. "Do you feel better? After the detox?"

"I feel as though a weight has lifted from me," I admitted. "It was joyous. To be honest, I'm still unsure if I'm just imagining all of this. It's like a dream."

"It's real," said Jodi. "See!" She grabbed my arm and pinched my skin.

"Ow!" I laughed. "Okay, okay, I believe!"

"Good. Now, let's have a cup of tea. This is exciting. I can't wait to get started now."

Jodi's enthusiasm was infectious and a relief; the women I'd had to work with at Barry's garden centre had no real interest in the plants and had been hard work to get along with. Barry himself was only interested in making money and had filled the shop with the usual plastic rubbish and resin statuary.

"Great idea," I agreed. "I'm parched."

As I waited for the kettle to boil, I took the broom propped up against the wall and began to sweep the floor. Dust eddied in the morning sunlight as it streamed through the window and warmed the air. The floor was laid with bricks, but they were in pretty good condition, as were the walls, and there was no evidence of damp. All the place needed was a good clean to rid it of dust and spiders' webs and it would be ready for fitting out with shelves and cupboards. The door needed some attention, but a carpenter could easily fix that.

The kettle boiled and as Jodi made the tea, I allowed myself to relax into the room's energy, surprised at my emotions. I felt more at home here after one day than I had ever done at the house I shared with Gerald. For the first time thoughts of Gerald didn't prick at me and his memory vanished as quickly as it had appeared. The heartache that had usually accompanied those memories didn't rise either. I gave the floor a final brush then rested the broom back against the wall and took the offered mug of tea. Steam rose into the air, the light catching as sparkles. Everything, even rising steam, seemed brushed with magic.

I sighed then took a sip of tea. "So," I said as Jodi leant up against the table sipping her own tea, "There is one thing I want to do."

"Oh?"

"Yes. I want to test my energy. I didn't make Cosimo flinch this morning, but if I'm still toxic ..."

"We can visit Cosimo. See if he'll let you stroke him?"

"Yesterday, at work, Beatrice made me touch a fern. It crumbled under my touch. Even Barry saw it."

"Barry?"

"My old boss." I had a distinct memory of him, loppers in hand, viciously hacking at the honeysuckle.

Jodi held up a hand. "My! You are powerful. I got a distinct wave of energy from you then. I'm not surprised that the fern died under your touch!"

"Seriously?"

She nodded. "Some witches have it, others don't, well not so intense. Or at least, I think they learn to control it. Aelfwen is fiery when she wants to be, but I don't get that sense of energy from her, even when she's in a mood, but you, wowzer, that was intense! Try to think happy thoughts when you touch the plants."

Killing plants with my negative energy was the last things I wanted. "I'll be a pretty terrible gardener if I keep killing the plants," I said remembering the sorry state of the plants back at garden centre. Had I really caused them to wilt and die off? I loved plants, had always been fascinated by their beauty. Each one was a living miracle, evidence that the universe had a power that the Barries of this world would never appreciate.

"You can learn to keep it under control and then you can turn it to work for the good."

I nodded. "I'll have to. I'd rather not be the grim reaper of the plant world."

Jodi made a nervous laugh and averted her eyes.

"Did I say something out of order?"

"Like what?" she asked.

Her ignorance was feigned. Whatever I had said had caused a reaction but just as I was about to dig a little more, Aelfwen walked through the door.

"Ah," she said. "The room feels very ... very at ease today."

"She's happy," Jodi said with a nod towards me. "Cosimo didn't make a fuss this morning, and she likes it here."

"Ah, good. Very good."

"And I think she likes Maximus."

"I do not. I never said that." A flush crept to my cheeks as Aelfwen threw me a questioning look. "I've only met him once-"

"Thrice!" Jodi threw back. "In the lane, at the pond, and in the courtyard—just now."

"He's my boss, Jodi."

"That's correct," agreed Aelfwen.

"Well, you said he needs-"

"Jodi, what I said was that he needs help—in the garden, which is exactly why Leofe is here."

"Okay," Jodie exuded mischievous energy. "As you like."

Chapter Sixteen

The rest of the day was spent with Aelfwen, now dressed in jeans and walking boots, giving me a tour of the gardens and outlining my responsibilities. There were acres to be maintained, which was a huge undertaking, but alongside Jodi there were two more gardeners Aldred and his son Drew, neither of whom were under fifty years of age.

"Much of the estate is laid to woodlands, and we have several fields that we rent out to local farmers. It's mostly sheep, but we do have a herd of cows in residence at the moment."

"The bull is in the next field. All alone, poor thing," said Jodi.

"Well, that's not our concern. The farmer is-"

"Lonely, like Maximus," she sighed and cast a glance my way.

Aelfwen's only response was to shake her head and continue to explain how the estate worked, and my role in it. "You really don't have to worry about overseeing the estate, Leofe, I deal with the farmers, and the woodsman who manages the woodland."

"Oh, you'll like him, Leofe. He lives in this amazing house in the woods. He's single too. Although I'm not sure if he's divorced or ever been married."

"Oh."

"Jodi, I'm quite sure that Leofe isn't interested in whether Wyman is single or not. Leofe, forgive Jodi," Aelfwen threw her a meaningful stare, "she's meddling where she ought not."

"That's alright, Aelfwen, I'm getting used to her."

"Well, I'm glad you see it that way. She berates me for not having a 'social filter', but really, I think it is she who ought to have one."

The tour continued and we moved from garden room to garden room. From my apartment window, I had seen that the gardens were extensive but set out in a formal pattern. Beyond the gardens was a band of open grassland given over to grazing land for sheep and, beyond that, woodlands appeared to stretch beyond the horizon. The estate was large, and the formal gardens huge by any normal standards, but they were organized and appeared manageable with a good team on board. One thing was for certain, with the numerous hedges, shrubs, and borders to maintain, my working day would be long and tiring. I would be consumed by planting schedules, pruning, sowing, and mulching, I would also be responsible for designing new areas that would interest visitors and investing in new plants. It would be hard work. I would be in heaven.

We reached the gravelled pathway that led to the poison garden. Either side, hedging had been planted and allowed to grow tall and wide and the pathway to the garden had narrowed to single file. At the front, now recessed among the leaves, was the metal sign that I had seen from my apartment. In white lettering on a black background it read, 'Poison Garden'. Beneath that was the universal sign for poison, a skull placed above crossed bones.

"But your most important role, Leofe," Aelfwen said as we stood at the head of the path, "will be as Guardian of the Poison Garden."

'Guardian' was an unusual way to frame my role but matched how I felt. I wanted to be a guardian of the natural world, someone in tune with the earth, nurturing it, rather than working against it or mining it. I didn't see myself as an eco-warrior but felt that Man's relationship with the earth was out of sync and in my own small way, I could help to change that.

Aelfwen led the way, pulling out an oversized iron key as we approached the gate at the bottom of the path. The change in energy was subtle but became distinct as I took the final steps to stand before the locked gate. At least nine feet high, it was attached to an ornate iron frame that disappeared either side into the surrounding overgrown hedges.

"The iron fence encircles the entire garden, but you can only see the structure from within. The only way into the garden is either through this gate or by climbing over the top."

"And then you'd rip your trousers—the hedge has enormous thorns."

I noticed the dog roses and briars within the hedge that circled the garden. "You really don't want people to get in here."

"It's poisonous."

"It's what gets out that's the problem," Jodi murmured.

Aelfwen threw her a glance then held up the key. "For you, as Keeper of the Poison Garden. Do you accept?"

"I-" I stalled, glanced through the gate to the gravel paths, neatly laid beds, arbours, and arches within. I sensed that accepting the key held a significance I could barely perceive. A wren hopped from an overhanging branch and into the ivy-laced hedge. "Yes!" I said as both women waited, "I accept."

Aelfwen and Jodi sighed in unison and the key was placed across my palm. At least five inches long, it was surprisingly heavy.

"Solid iron," Aelfwen explained. "Forged especially for this lock." She pointed to the gate. "And now, trusted to you, one of only two in existence."

"Are you sure I should keep it?"

"Absolutely. You must. You are the Keeper now."

"You are," Jodi agreed.

"Shall we?" Aelfwen urged with a sweep of her arm towards the gate.

The key tingled against my skin, and a distinct pulse of energy emanated from the garden as I slid it into the lock. The gate unlocked with ease, but as I pushed it open, I sensed tension. It wasn't coming from Aelfwen or Jodi. It was in the air, and I felt it as a pressure. Energy was being held back as it pushed against invisible barriers but as I stepped over the threshold, the tension disappeared.

"Ah!" sighed Aelfwen. "All is well."

She walked behind me until we reached an area wide enough for us to stand together and then took my hand. Her eyes glittered. Watching the emerald of her iris sparkle, I was transfixed. "Welcome, Leofe Swinson, daughter of Ardith and Algar Swinson. Welcome Keeper of the Poison Garden, Guardian of the Gate."

"Assistant Guardian," Jodi corrected.

Aelfwen batted a hand at Leofe. "Don't spoil the moment, Jodi."

"Just saying, she's the assistant Guardian."

"Yes, of course, but not now."

"Assistant Guardian?"

"Yes, and the Keeper. You have the key, so you are the Keeper."

"But you said assistant. So, who is the main guardian?"

"Why Maximus, of course."

"Tsk! Jodi, little by little. You're making things difficult for me."

The key tingled in my hand and an odd sensation, as though a low voltage electrical current was being brushed against my skin, began at the back of my head then flowed across my shoulders, then down my arms, ending in my fingers. The tingle became intense at the tips and energy prickled between my fingers. A spark shot from my thumb. Yelping in surprise, I waved my hand in the air. "I'm on fire!"

"See what you've done, Jodi."

"How is it my fault?"

"You've confused the girl—made her anxious. The confluence of her energy and the garden's is too much for her. She isn't prepared."

They both watched as I continued to wave my hand but showed no sign of concern. The sparks were contagious and both hands were now sparking. "Help!"

"Oh, for Thor's sake!"

As the sparks grew to the intensity of a Bonfire Night sparkler, Aelfwen grabbed my hands and clapped them together. The sensation of being electrocuted was instant, but the sparking stopped. The scent of singed hair rose to my nostrils.

"What happened?" I gasped. "What just happened?"

"Now, look at me, Leofe. Be calm. Be still."

Aelfwen's voice was entirely soothing, and my racing heart slowed.

"Breathe. Take a deep breath."

I took a deep breath.

"This," she raised our joined hands, "was a manifestation of your power—your inner magick. You're like your mother, Leofe, maybe more powerful. Poor Ardith tried so hard to fit into the ordinary world, to keep you safe, but she had more power in her little finger than many of us have in our entire selves. You, Leofe, are like her. The force is strong in you."

My mother had been a little eccentric, peculiar to some, but if she'd had magical powers and felt she had to hide them, it explained much of my chaotic childhood.

"Now." Aelfwen gently released my hands. "There is much that I must explain to you, and you have much to learn. In her efforts to protect you, Ardith, in some ways, did you a disservice, but never mind that now. The problem we face is that your power is learning to release itself from its bonds, but you do not have the knowledge of how to control it. You will learn that over the coming weeks."

The tingling sensation became painful prickling on my palms.

"Did you do as I asked, and bring your mother's herbal with you?"

"Yes, it's in the apartment," I said distracted by the burning sensation, worried that my hands would burst back into fireworks.

"Wonderful. There is much within its pages that you must learn.

I waved my hands in the air in the hope of relieving the prickling pain.

"Just remember to stay calm," counselled Aelfwen. "Now, the book?"

"I've had a flick through—there's lots of recipes, but some of the earlier stuff is written in a language I can't read."

"That knowledge will come in time."

The wren I'd watched hop from the overhanging branch to the hedge, returned to the branch and chittered just as a magpie flew down from a large oak that sat just beyond the garden. The magpie ignored the wren and eyed me then hopped closer. As it took another leap forward, landing on the budding stem of a growing foxglove, a squirrel ran across the gravel path only feet from me then expertly scurried to the top of an archway. It sat on the cross bar and waited. All three seemed to be watching me, unafraid. Two crows swooped low and joined the magpie. The squirrel chittered and the magpie responded with a squawk.

"Are they tame?" I asked as the creatures continued to sit and watch.

"No, they're wild, but very nosey."

Another squirrel bolted from the circling hedge and ran up the arbour to join the first. The squirrel chittered to its companion then both turned their attention back to us.

"This is weird. They seem to be waiting for something. Should we feed them?"

"We can reward them later. They are here because they're nosey, they've come to see the new Guardian."

It was a nice conceit, but I wasn't buying into it, no doubt one of the gardeners fed the animals and they were expecting some breakfast. "Well, I guess if they're not hissing and spitting at me, that's progress."

"Certainly, the detoxification ceremony worked," agreed Aelfwen.

I took a step to the squirrels, fascinated. This was the closest I had ever been to one. They chittered excitedly to one another, then shimmied down the pole and ran back across the gravel before disappearing into the hedge.

"You're a regular Cinderella," laughed Jodi. "The mice will be making you breakfast before you know it."

I laughed at this picture. "With my luck, I'd be befriended by rats!"

Aelfwen joined in the laughter then took a step towards the cottage. "Leofe, can you fetch your mother's grimoire, and I will explain some of your duties here in the poison garden."

"Grimoire?"

"Yes, the herbal."

"Isn't a grimoire a book full of spells?"

"Indeed," she smiled.

To my knowledge, my mother's book was full of recipes for salves and lotions and details about what herbs were poisonous, which beneficial, which were good for your health. If Aelfwen thought that it was filled with spells, she was going to be disappointed. "Sure," I said. "I'll fetch it."

"Lovely. Jodi will have a cup of tea waiting for you. All this walking and talking has made me thirsty."

I agreed and left the garden to fetch the book, sure that Aelfwen would be disappointed, and walked back to the house.

As I reached the terrace, I heard voices and then Maximus appeared. By his side was a woman. Tall and slender, her blonde hair glinting in the sunlight, arm slipped across his back, her laughter carried in the air as he spoke. Oblivious of my presence, they walked in unison towards me. I unhooked the latch without noise and slipped inside, surprised at the knot of pain in my belly and the flash of resentment I felt towards the woman. 'You like him. You think he's handsome.' Jodi's voice rang in my thoughts. *Just shut up! He's my boss. Nothing more. He's arrogant too and he obviously likes fake women!* And he certainly wasn't as lonely as Jodi had suggested.

Chapter Seventeen

When I returned to the Poison Garden, Aelfwen and Jodi were waiting for me at the picturesque cottage. Two small, multi-paned windows sat either side of a surprisingly large and heavy door. Its grass-covered roof almost reached the ground and sods of turf were stacked beneath and around the sides. A stonework chimney protruded from the far end of the roof from where, yesterday, smoke had risen. With its steeply pitched roof covered in grass and wooden frontage, it resembled a Viking turf house.

"This is Poison Garden HQ," Aelfwen beamed and clicked the latch. The door swung open a fraction and she gestured for me to step inside. "Keeper first," she smiled.

My hesitation lasted only a moment; I had wanted to see inside the cottage from the moment I noticed it from my apartment window. I was not disappointed.

Tardis-like, the interior of the one-room cottage was much larger than I expected. At the far end sat a large stone-built fireplace. A heavy mantel marked the top of the hearth and intricate designs of intertwined birds were carved into the stone. Within the hearth, stones had been piled either side and an iron grille placed upon them. A deep pile of ashes lay beneath. Above the grille hung a pot-bellied iron pot. Held aloft by a large metal arm attached to one side of the chimney's wall, and blackened with soot, it resembled a cauldron.

A series of posts used to hold up the roof were also used as dividers within the room. One section was given over to a Welsh dresser, the shelves stacked with leather bound books and glass jars. The cupboard top held an array of jars and a large wicker trug filled with wooden-handled garden tools. A pair of bright tan leather gloves had been laid neat and shiny on top of the tools. They looked unused, as did the half-apron hung from a peg on the post beside the dresser.

Aelfwen picked up the gloves. "Most of the tools here have been used for decades, some for centuries, but we thought that you'd like something new for yourself." She held out the tan leather gloves.

"Thank you."

Light filtered in through the window at the roof's apex.

Beside the dresser, in the next 'alcove' was a wide seat constructed between two beams. A large flat cushion sat atop a wooden base, and this was covered with a sheep's fleece. It resembled a day bed. Hung behind it was a large cow's hide. In the opposite alcove was a wooden desk and chair and beside that another table held a kettle and several tin cannisters. Hung behind it on the wall was a small shelf unit with cups and plates. Beneath it was a small fridge.

"You've got all mod cons here, Leofe," Aelfwen explained as she opened the fridge to show an immaculately clean interior and a single bottle of milk. She pulled it out and then flicked the switch on the kettle. "Make yourself at home; this is your office now."

As she busied herself making a pot of tea, I took time to explore the cottage, gravitating towards the large dresser and its shelves stacked with books and jars. There were numerous books on botany and several that explored the uses of plants. There were several volumes in one series filled with botanical drawings of plants considered to be poisonous. Each plant was explored over several pages, their individual parts drawn with careful detail and labelled. Each set of drawings was followed by their uses, both healing and toxic, and explanations of symptoms of their poisoning. A final page listed recipes and the charms to be said during their preparation. Fascinated, I turned my attention to the jars. Most had the skull and crossbones printed on the labels and contained the dried leaves, stems and roots, or seeds of henbane, wolf's bane, hemlock, and digitalis.

"There's more in the cupboard below."

Opening the cupboard revealed shelves stacked with glass jars and several boxes filled with neatly placed bags. Each bag was labelled with its contents. "A seed bank," I said as I read the labels that recorded the name of the plant and date of collection.

"Yes, we've been collecting them for a number of years. We send them all over the world. We'd like to have the biggest collection of poisonous plants in the country, Marissa thinks it would be a real draw for visitors."

Jodi groaned.

"It's a controversial idea," Aelfwen stated.

"Who's Marissa?"

"Marissa is our marketing expert."

Jodi rolled her eyes.

"Don't you like her, Jodi?"

"Nope!" she shook her head. "She wants to get her talons into Maximus." She clawed a hand through the air and grimaced.

"Is she slim with blonde hair? A brash kind of loud laugh?" I asked remembering the blonde hugging Maximus to her side.

"You've seen her?"

"I think so. When I went to get my mother's book. Mr. Blackwood was walking with a woman. They went into the Hall."

Jodi groaned again. "She's back."

"She's here for a meeting, Jodi."

"Please tell me that I don't have to attend!"

"You don't have to attend."

This response was met with a relieved sigh from Jodi.

Aelfwen poured tea into three mugs, added milk, then passed them around. "But it would be useful if you could come to the meeting, Leofe. I know that Maximus wants to speak to you, and we'd appreciate your input."

"Me?"

Aelfwen nodded whilst throwing a reassuring smile.

"I'm not sure I'll be any use," I protested. "I don't know anything about marketing."

"No, but you've worked in botanical gardens and nurseries and garden centres, I'm sure you have a sense of what the customers like."

"I guess," I shrugged then took a sip of tea. "The garden centres I worked in were ... well, they were nothing like this place," I said glancing around the wooden beams of the cottage and noticing the huge spiders' webs that clung there. "They were filled with a lot of plastic urns and resin statues, garden gnomes and the like. The nursery was better—that really focused on the plants. I guess the botanical garden is the closest. I loved it there too."

"Well, you can make some suggestions, I'm sure. What we don't want is for this place to be turned into a kind of theme park. Marissa has been trying to talk Maximus into turning some of the outhouses into burger bars! She's even tried suggesting that we look for investors and create a theme park within the woods." Aelfwen shuddered. "Can you imagine, tearing down the woodlands and building a fairground there?"

"It would be dreadful!" Jodi said with feeling.

"It would, but it's what a lot of the stately homes have done. I guess they need the revenue."

"Well, we shall just have to find the revenue from elsewhere. It's a difficult path to tread. The Hall needs to be kept in good repair, and that takes money, but we cannot turn it over to the public en-masse."

Jodi shuddered. "All that bad energy flowing around the place!"

"I agree, it would be terrible, but that's where you come in, Leofe."

"Oh?"

"Yes, we want to open the gardens to the public—on select occasions, and perhaps allow the Hall to be used for weddings – sometimes – but we need to bring the place up to muster."

"That's something I can definitely help with. And obviously, the poison garden will be a draw."

"Oh! No. Not the Poison Garden. They cannot come here."

"No?" I asked confused at the heat of her reaction.

"Nope," Jodi agreed.

"The garden is very ... special." She glanced at her watch. "Well, now is really not the time to go into this. Maximus has requested that you go to his office, and you may already be late."

"What?"

Chapter Eighteen

Ten minutes later, heart fluttering, I stood outside Maximus'
office with my clenched fist raised to knock on the door. The
thought of attending the marketing meeting had been bad
enough but having to face the man who had seen me in my
birthday suit was making the palms of my hands sweat. If he'd
been like Barry, my old boss, then I'm pretty sure I'd take the
ordeal in my stride, but Maximus wasn't an overweight forty-
something with a balding pate and a nasty habit of snorting
back phlegm then spitting it out wherever he stood. No, Maximus was the Jason Mamoa of the stately home world. Bearded,
and over six feet tall, he was broad-shouldered and muscular
with dark hair grown long. Sure, he showed the signs of
age—crow's feet around his eyes, greying streaks in his beard
and at his temples, but that just added to the man's charismatic
presence. And then there were the eyes, amber edging towards
topaz, outlined by the darkest of black lashes, that held me in
their gaze as our eyes locked!

Whoa! You like him!

No!

But you're dreaming about him!

*Well ... it was just a dream, and I can be forgiven for having
weird dreams after the day I'd had. And anyway, he's my boss and
arrogant with it so off limits.*

My raised hand remained stalled.

Just calm down.

I took a calming breath. It helped ease some tension.

Let's be honest, there is no way he would be interested in you anyway, and if you think you can compete with glamorous consultants like Marissa then you really are deluded.

I have no intention of competing with her. He's my boss and I'm not interested anyway. It would be stupid to even think a man like that would be interested in me—divorced, rejected, returned goods, remember!

I knocked on the door.

"Come in!"

Gazing out of the window to the garden below, Maximus turned to me as I entered. Closing the door gave me a moment to take a breath before facing him. The heat of a nervous flush had already begun to spread at the base of my throat. *Why had I agreed to go into the pond!*

"Mistress Swinson!" He offered me a broad smile. The crow's feet at the side of his eyes crinkled. Topaz eyes framed by dark lashes took me in. There was the hint of amusement in them. Prickles began to sting my cheeks. *Calm down. It will be over soon.*

Unlike Barry, Maximus did not check me out from head to toe, but instead held my gaze and gestured for me to sit on the chair before his desk. It was a good start. Barry had always revulsed me with his letch-like gaze as it travelled down my body, resting on my boobs then travelling below my waistline. I'd quickly taken to wearing baggy jumpers switching to generous cotton shirts at the height of summer.

I lowered myself onto the leather chair and perched on its edge, still too anxious to relax; this was my first 'meeting' with my new boss after all. I offered a smile that I hoped would be professional, glad that I hadn't begun weeding the large patch of hemlock that I'd marked out as my first job that afternoon.

"How are you settling in?" He sat down in the oversized chair opposite and relaxed back against its buttoned leather back, the picture of easy confidence. The gleam in his topaz eyes remained. "What do you think to your apartment?"

"Oh, well, it's wonderful," I said with genuine pleasure.

He nodded. "Good. And the house? It suits you?"

"Well ... it's beautiful."

"It was built in 1573 by my Uncle Mattias. There's a painting of him in the gallery. I shall show it to you one day. He came over from Europe when the family had troubles ..." He gazed at the ceiling as though lost in thought. "But I digress. You don't want to hear a potted history of my family."

"I'm sure it's fascinating." *Although how could he be your uncle if the house was built in 1573?*

"Well, anyway—another time. So, Mistress Aelfwen has explained your duties ... and your Guardianship of the poison garden?"

"Yes. She's explained you're keen on holding events and would like to make the Poison Garden seed library world renowned."

"Indeed," he nodded. "And your Guardianship? She has explained that?"

"Assistant Guardian."

"Yes, assistant."

"It was mentioned."

"And you agreed to become the Keeper of the Poison Garden?"

I nodded.

"You took the key?"

"Yes."

"And the garden accepted you?"

"Erm ... yes."

"Good!" At this news he clapped his hands, stood and walked back to the window.

I waited patiently but he made no effort to speak and only looked through the window to the garden.

Was that it? Was I free to go?

"So, I'll go then," I said rising from my seat.

Maximus continued to stare out of the window.

Bloody cheek! Insufferable! Dismissed, and more certain that my original judgement that Maximus Blackwood was arrogant was correct, I turned to leave.

"Oh, Mistress Swinson-"

"It's just Leofe," I returned without a smile, irked by his dismissive attitude. He wasn't only arrogant, he was rude too!

"Leofe, then." He forced a smile. "I'd like to speak to you later. Come back here this evening, after supper."

Yes, sir! "Is seven o'clock too late?"

Topaz eyes caught mine once more, the mirthful gleam gone. "That's fine."

At that moment the door swung open, only narrowly missing my shoulder.

"Maximus! I-" Marissa entered in full flow, stopping as she noticed me then glanced across at Maximus before casting a questioning then dismissive look my way. Within less than a second the narrowing of her eyes, and thinning of her lips, was replaced by a forced smile. She strode into the room, pushing past me.

"Maximus!" she repeated as she stood in between us. "Did you receive my email? I've had some exciting news."

He grunted in return, and I closed the door behind me, shutting out Marissa's overly enthusiastic and domineering voice. The woman's brash energy grated on me, and I returned to the poison garden with relief whilst dreading having to attend the 'marketing' meeting Aelfwen had organized for later in the afternoon.

Chapter Nineteen

Notebook in hand, I wandered around the Poison Garden. So far, of all the garden rooms I had seen at the Hall, this was the one I liked the most. Unable to keep the smile from my face, I moved from bed to bed discovering what each contained, glancing back at my 'office' at regular intervals marvelling at how my life had changed within a matter of days. Helping to make the Poison Garden world renowned and the 'go to' repository for seeds was a project I was more than happy to help make a reality. I moved from bed to bed, entering the details of each plant and its position on the roughly drawn map I had sketched into the notebook. I intended to make a large map of the garden and hang it on the wall above my desk. This would help me not only familiarize myself with the garden but also keep track of each plant, its health, sowing, planting, harvesting times etcetera. So far, the list of poisonous plants was impressive and included some of the deadliest I knew of. We had beds of hemlock, wolfsbane, mandrake, henbane, and belladonna, and an impressive colony of fly agaric, the red and white capped toadstools that looked so cute but were deadly poisonous. Most were capable of causing death, vomiting, hallucinations, and coma. There were several plants I didn't recognize and for which I could find no label and I made a note of these and their position on the sketched map.

We were heading towards June, and the heat from the afternoon sun had become intense. Sweat trickled at my temple. I needed a hat, and I really should have put sunscreen on. I decided to return to the office, make myself a cup of tea, and take a break until the sun was less intense when Jodi entered the garden. She held a trug filled with roses and waved as she noticed me.

"Hey, Leofe!" she called from the gate and took quick steps forward. Already tanned from the summer sun and dressed in a white shirt tied at the waist with sleeves rolled up, capri style blue jeans, and white plimsolls, she exuded the light and carefree air of youth. As she lifted her sunglasses, violet eyes without a hint of crow's feet, smiled.

"Hi!" I replied. "I was just about to go inside. The sun's getting to me."

"It is!" she exclaimed. "You're as red as a beetroot. Are you hot? You look sweaty."

"Thanks!" I laughed but wiped at my temple covering the back of my hand with a film of moisture. "I am a bit hot, but don't burn easily."

"You sure?"

"Yes," I laughed. "I tan, but generally don't burn."

"You do look like you've caught the sun though."

"Well, I was about to go inside to escape from it."

"Tea?"

I nodded and she followed me to the office and filled the kettle.

"What do you think of Marissa?" she asked.

"She seems nice enough," I answered, taken by surprise at Jodi's bluntness. "Very professional." The 'marketing' meeting had been as I expected. Marissa domineered the conversation, taking no interest in any suggestions that any of the other staff members had made. Maximus though polite, simply listened. It was an uncomfortable half hour, and I was glad to leave.

"Knows her own mind," I said with my best effort at diplomacy.

"Hmm. Do you think she's pretty?"

"Well, I guess so."

"She has nice dresses."

"I hadn't noticed," I lied.

"She makes a lot of effort, I think, to look nice. I mean she's old, a bit like you, but she looks good. I'm not that keen on her, she's too bossy for my liking and she's definitely making a play for Maximus, but she does make an effort ... with the way she dresses." She said this whilst cocking her head and looking at me.

She thinks that I don't make an effort!

"You wore that yesterday, didn't you?" She gestured to my outfit; a favourite *Iron Maiden* t-shirt I'd bought at a concert years ago and blue jeans that were wearing thin at the knee. "Well, I packed light, and I am working in a garden so there's no point in me tottering about in heels and a pencil skirt!"

"No, but ... I mean, I bet if you got your hair done, you'd look really nice."

"You don't like my hair?"

"Oh, yes, I mean no, that's not what I meant. What I mean is that it's kind of long. Has it been a long time since you had it cut?"

Aelfwen was right; Jodi had no social filter. She wasn't wrong though. I tried to remember the last time I'd visited the hairdresser but failed. "I can't remember when it was."

"There's a good hairdresser in town, they could do it for you, maybe add a few highlights, to cover up the grey."

"I like my grey!"

"Sure, but it would make you look younger—more like Marissa's age."

"Really."

"Yes, and they could look at your eyebrows too."

"What's wrong with my eyebrows?"

"Oh, nothing! It's just, I don't think monobrows are in this season."

"What? I do *not* have a monobrow."

"Well, just a little one."

I rubbed at the space between my brows.

"And ...," she rubbed a finger across her top lip.

Unable to resist, I stroked the skin at the side of my lip. Hairs, far more wiry than I had ever felt had sprung up close to the corner of my mouth.

"See?"

I nodded.

"Marissa doesn't have those."

I was becoming sick of hearing that woman's name! "Well, I'm a kind of low maintenance gal!" I joked.

"More like no maintenance!"

I wasn't sure how to react. There was something naïve and endearing about Jodi. She *was* being more personal than was comfortable, but I didn't get a sense that she was trying to disparage or mock me. Plus, Jodi had a point. Over the years, I hadn't exactly let myself go, and I'd lost some of the weight I'd put on during the lonelier years of my marriage but since discovering Gerald's bigamy I'd made no effort with my appearance. My mind drifted back to the kitchen when I'd caught myself reflected in the window, hair scraped back and taking a swig of wine from the bottle. I'd looked slim, but scraggy. I realized it had been years since I'd had my hair cut and many months since I'd bothered to even look at my eyebrows.

"Tomorrow's Saturday," Jodi continued. "Why don't you go into town and take a look around." Her violet eyes sparkled as she threw me a warm smile.

The kettle began to boil, and I turned to make the tea. "Maybe," I replied although I had little to zero interest in going into town and being pampered and powdered. I had a pair of tweezers among my toiletries; I'd sort my face out in the evening.

"Good! And maybe you can buy some new clothes? Something a little more feminine and ... colourful. Less skulls, blood, and demons?"

Chapter Twenty

Orange light hit the back wall as early evening sun shone through the apartment windows. I breathed in the atmosphere of the room. Like the air, it was warm and soothing, and I shut the door against the world with a smile. My stomach growled. The afternoon had been a flood of new information as I discovered more about the poison garden. I'd finished my workday with a walk around the larger gardens then made my way to the courtyard. Cosimo, Maximus' chestnut stallion had leant his head over the stable door, allowing me to stroke his nose and pat his neck. I was forgiven for scaring him in the lane and the detox had obviously worked.

Placing the apartment keys on the table, I made my way to the kitchen. A note had been left on the counter. 'Dinner in the fridge. Coq Au Vin. Reheat for 20 minutes. 180'. In the fridge was a covered glass bowl. I made a cup of tea as the food cooked then relaxed in the living room, wallowing in the lowering sun's orange light, and waited. Exhausted by the day, my eyes began to lower and with the aroma of coq au vin rising in the kitchen, the image of Maximus holding me in his gaze as the stallion reared, I sank down into sleep.

I woke to the insistent and high-pitched beep of a fire alarm and smoke filtering into the living room. In the kitchen, smoke seeped from the cooker door and the siren grew piercing. I pushed the window open then turned my attention to the cooker, turning it off at the wall. A kitchen chair served as a ladder and I pushed the fire alarm's button to switch off the insistent, ear-splitting beep.

Smoke billowed into the room as I opened the cooker door and wafted it towards the open window. As the cloud of smoke cleared, I noticed the clock on the wall. It read twenty-five minutes past seven o'clock. Maximus wanted to see me at seven! The next few minutes were a blur of hasty preparations to make myself look less like the complete mess I was. There was no time to change so instead I splashed my face with water. The mirror reflected a middle-aged woman, flushed and reddened by the sun, with hair scraped back in an unflattering ponytail in wispy, just-got-out-of-bed disarray. With no time to make a reasonable effort at improving my appearance, I splashed my face with cooling water, dabbed it dry, then ran from the apartment, slowing down only to release my hair from the ponytail.

I arrived outside of Maximus' office breathing heavily. I took a moment to compose myself then knocked at the door. It swung open just as my knuckles hit the wood.

"Oh!" He stood before me magnificent! Six foot four of bearded alpha male, impressive in a perfectly fitted jacket over a white shirt that couldn't hide his muscular chest. In that moment I wanted him more than any man I had ever wanted before. Stunned at the overwhelming shot of desire that gripped me as his topaz eyes locked to mine, my heart skipped a beat.

"Ah, Leofe, you're here."

"I am." It was the most coherent reply I could manage.

He continued to hold my gaze. A questioning frown. "Are you alright? You seem a little out of breath and ... a little red. Have you caught the sun today? You should be careful; too much sun will make your wrinkles worse."

Did he just say that? I must look a sight! I touched a finger to the skin beside my eyes. It felt hot to the touch. "I am," *I repeat-*

ed. He stared at me whilst waiting for a reply; excruciating moments passed. "I mean ... well ..." *You're a hot mess!* Pushing fingers through hair that still straggled over my shoulders, I apologized for being late without explaining that I'd managed to destroy my evening meal and nearly smoke the apartment out. "I've been busy ... time got away with me."

"And you forgot about me?"

"Oh, no! No, I didn't forget about you, I ..."

He chuckled and opened the door. "Come in. We need to talk, you and I."

I followed him into the office, noticing how good he looked from behind in his dinner suit. It fit him perfectly. *Dinner suit?* So, he was getting ready to go out.

He turned, leaning against the desk. The top button of his immaculate shirt remained open. A silk tie in darkest red hung either side of his collar.

"So, Leofe ..."

"Yes?"

"How are you settling in?"

How to answer that question? I didn't ever want to leave, so pretty good, I guess. "So far so good," I replied. "I've been making notes about the plants in the poison garden and started to compile a list of the plants we don't have."

"Ah, good. Yes, Aelfwen is keen on collecting as many as possible. Marissa has bigger plans, as you heard this afternoon."

I only nodded. Maximus hadn't opposed any of Marissa's ideas, so I presumed he agreed with her. If that was the case, the estate may attract more visitors, but lose much of its character.

"You don't approve?"

Had he read my thoughts? "Approve?"

"Of Marissa's plans."

"Oh, well, it's difficult for me to say. I've only been here a couple of days. She may be right that turning an area of woodland into a Tree Top Activity Centre would attract visitors. And I guess that turning one of the wings into a haunted house or escape room experience might draw visitors too."

"But you don't like that idea?"

"Well, I think turning Blackwood Hall into a Gothic theme park (*is appalling*) is ... different, but it may work."

"You don't sound convinced."

"I'm not. I mean ... it's not my area of expertise. I'm a gardener, I'm afraid I don't know much about marketing."

"But you do know about gardens and just how ... special they can be. The Poison Garden is so much more than a collection of plants just as Blackwood Hall is so much more than a pile of bricks built into a house."

"It is!"

He smiled. "And the garden accepted you."

This was an odd phrase. "Accepted me?"

"Yes. When you crossed the threshold, the garden accepted you as the Keeper. You are the Guardian of the Poison Garden now."

"Assistant Guardian, apparently."

He nodded without evidence of mirth, a frown forming. "Yes, assistant."

"I'll do my best to help it thrive and make it world renowned."

He appeared surprised by my response. "But you will be the Guardian?"

"I'll do my best."

His frown deepened then he pushed up from the desk, muttering. The words were unintelligible to me, possibly in a language I did not understand. He had mentioned that his family had come over from Europe. What had I said that was so wrong? "I'm really keen to help," I tried.

He nodded. "I see."

"So, I've drawn up a list ..."

"A list ... yes."

Again, the wrong thing to say. I was getting nowhere and obviously disappointing him. Increasingly uneasy, what confidence I had slipping, I tried a different tactic. "Mr Blackwood, what exactly are my duties as Assistant Guardian?"

"So Aelfwen has not explained to you."

"She said you want the Poison Garden to be world renowned. Or, rather, Marissa does."

"Nothing else?"

"Nothing else that wasn't already in the job description you advertised."

He considered me for a moment then, with obvious irritation, said, "Well, I'm afraid that we are wasting our time and it grows late. As you can see, I am ready to go out."

I was dismissed! Again. *Fine!* "Am I free to go?" I asked, irked by his curtness.

Again, he seemed surprised. Topaz eyes held mine. "You are, but first I would like you to do me a favour."

You dismiss me with a flick of your hand, but you want my help? The master/servant relationship was well entrenched. "If I can."

"My tie." He held the ends of the dark red tie in his hands, a flicker of uncertainty passing over his eyes. His smile lacked its usual confidence. "I'm no good at it. All fingers and thumbs." Just like his frame, his hands were large. He held my gaze for several moments.

"Sure." I tried to appear unflustered despite the sudden racing of my heart; helping with his tie meant standing close, very close. "I used to tie Gerald's, not that he wore ties often though." *Why are you talking about your ex? Stay calm. Don't make a fool of yourself. He's your boss!* I reached for the ends of the silk tie. Maximus lifted his chin. Heat from his body stroked the back of my hands, and my fingers began to prickle. *Calm down!* The last time I'd felt this way my hands had erupted like a sparkler on Bonfire Night and setting fire to my new boss would not go down well, I was sure. *Take a breath. Breathe!*

"Gerald?"

"Shall I do the top button up?"

"Uhuh."

"My very much ex-husband," I explained, hands tingling.

"Oh, I'm sorry."

"No need to be. I'm not. He was a lousy husband. It just took me thirty years to realise it." I managed a wry laugh.

Maximus chuckled. "You're lucky then."

"How so?" I asked as I reached up to take hold of his collar. His skin was warm against my fingers as they brushed against his neck. He shivered beneath my touch.

The air between us filled with particles of his scent. "Sorry! Did I scratch you?"

"No! It ... sometimes it takes longer."

"It'll only take a minute or so."

"No, finding out you're married to the wrong person."

"Oh, yes, but longer than thirty years?"

"For me it was longer."

You were married? Who to? What was she like? Are you older than me? Did you marry younger? I managed to laugh in a good humoured way despite the flood of questions firing in my brain. "I guess we're both better off single then."

"Aye." He agreed, chin still raised.

With the collar now buttoned, I took the ends of the tie in hand but, just as I began to cross one end over the other, the door opened.

"Well, well, well! What's going on here then?"

I turned to see Marissa striding across the floor in a red, figure-hugging dress that accentuated her curvaceous figure. She made a b-line for us. Clusters of diamantes twinkled at her shoulders and a glittering belt accentuated her slender waist. Glossy golden hair bounced on her naked shoulders. Within seconds she was nudging me out of the way. "I'll take over from here," she said as she placed her hands over mine and gripped the tie. Maximus' addictive scent was obliterated by her overpowering and cloying perfume.

Taken by surprise by her heavy-handed effort to take my place, I released the tie. "Sure."

Maximus made no effort to stop her, and with her back to me, she deftly knotted the tie. "There," she said as she brushed invisible lint from his suit. "You're ready." She turned and slipped her arm through Maximus'. Despite her smile, her eyes narrowed as she rested her free hand on his bicep—the human equivalent of a male cat spraying its territory.

It was ridiculous! I was no threat to her; there was no way I could compete.

"What is that smell?" she asked whilst looking straight at me. She took a step forward, sniffing at the air. "It's you. You smell of ... smoke!"

I realized then that not only was I red-faced and sweaty, but I stank of the smoke that had billowed out of the oven too. I scrambled for an explanation, not wanting to out myself for nearly setting the house on fire. "We were burning leaves. I haven't had time to change." My cheeks, already warm, began to tingle.

She raised a perfectly manicured brow. "Oh."

"Leofe has been working hard all day," Maximus smiled. "I'm sure she's ready for a peaceful evening at home. We don't want to keep her any longer," he said, taking a step forward.

"Absolutely not," Marissa agreed. "And if we don't leave soon, we're going to be late and if there's one thing Arabella Glaxwell-Smythe hates it is guests being late to one of her charitable balls."

Maximus groaned. "Excuse us, Leofe. Duty awaits."

Gladly! "No problem," I replied. "I've got a busy evening ahead, myself," I lied and turned to leave.

"I hope it includes having a bath."

Marissa's tinkling laugh fell like daggers along my spine, and the painful tingling at my fingertips increased but instead of turning to confront her I took increasingly rapid steps out of the office.

Back in my apartment, I closed the door behind me with relief. I spent the remainder of the evening making sure the kitchen was clean and smoke free then took a quick shower, washed my hair and, finally, sat in front of the fire. Hair drying, and soothed by the warmth, I lost myself in the flickering flames, pushing away thoughts of Maximus and Marissa. I had no doubt that what Jodi had said was true; Marissa wanted to get her claws into Maximus and, from what I witnessed tonight, they were sinking into him quite successfully. Well, they were welcome to each other. I would focus on my job. The flames grew low and rather than putting another log on the fire, I went to bed and fell to sleep imagining myself walking through the Poison Garden.

I awoke with a start, woken from a dream where a dark presence was following me around the garden. A woman shouted and then a door banged. This time, instead of investigating, I remained in bed. The sensation of being followed in my dream clung to me in those moments but quickly evaporated. As I slipped back into sleep, another series of thuds was followed by a cackling laugh, but already slipping below consciousness it was impossible to tell in which realm, the conscious or sub-conscious, they belonged.

Chapter Twenty-One

The following morning, the sun shone brilliant light through my apartment windows although clouds in the far distance held the promise of rain. Saturday was my day to do as I pleased, and I decided to explore the local town.

After a quick breakfast of scrambled eggs on toast and two cups of black tea, I dressed, grabbed my jacket and helmet, and made my way downstairs. The house was silent, and I met no one as I walked to the side gate and into the carpark where my bike remained after I'd returned from the near collision with Maximus and his horse. I made a mental note to ask if there was a shed or garage where I could keep the bike undercover. It was a vintage model and keeping it in working order took a little more effort than newer bikes, but I enjoyed the challenge and seeing it rust from being left out in the elements would hurt. If there was nowhere suitable then I'd have to buy a cover which was not ideal, but better than nothing.

It took twenty minutes of riding through twisting lanes before I came to open fields and passed the first sign for the local town. It took another ten to reach it. The town sat at the bottom of a series of undulating hills covered in fields of yellowing wheat. A wide river formed a boundary at its rear. Large houses, their boundaries softened by mature trees, lined the road on one side of the main road into town, a large park to the other. I followed the road to the town centre and found a small carpark. Twenty minutes later, thanks to a cancelled appointment, I sipped coffee as my hair was trimmed, layered, and shaped. Other appointments were made and by lunchtime

I had a new hairdo, manicured nails, expertly waxed brows, and an upper lip and chin devoid of hair. It was the first time I'd had any kind of vanity appointment for more than a year and it felt good. I left the salon with a smile, a bounce in my newly blown-dry hair, and a sense of renewal. The next stop was a boutique where I purchased two pairs of jeans which promised to 'shape and lift', a baby-pink cotton shirt that tied at the waist, and three close-fitting t-shirts in summery colours. With Barry out of my life, I was safe to wear what I wanted and not hide myself beneath baggy t-shirts and oversized hoodies to avoid his lecherous glances.

I left the boutique, bags in hand, and stopped. A woman I recognized immediately was crossing the road towards me. Cordelia! My stomach knotted. How could she be here? Seconds passed as I watched her approach, dread growing stronger. She was headed straight for me, and it wasn't until she was only feet away that I realized it wasn't her, just a woman who looked uncannily the same—a doppelganger. With my stomach now churning, she noticed my caught-in-headlights stare, frowned, and stepped onto the path before opening the boutique door and disappearing inside.

Unsettled and with hands trembling as the shot of adrenaline rode my veins, I made my way back to my bike and packed the bag in a pannier. Grey clouds loomed in the distance and from the direction of the wind, they would be passing this way soon. I figured I had about ten minutes before the rain clouds caught up with me. If I was lucky, I would be riding beneath the canopy of Blackwood Hall's woodland lanes by then. I set off with a purpose and pulled back the throttle as soon as I exited the town. Passing fields of golden wheat, I leaned into corners, opening up the bike on the straights. Clouds ran across the sky, and the sun cast a grey light. Wind began to buffet the bike and the first spatters of rain, large and heavy, fell on my shoulders. A steep hill gave way to a dip, and I swung into it, accelerating as the road swung to the left and then back up. Large droplets now beat against my helmet and visor, and I reached the woodlands just as the rain became torrential. Wet road turned to dry and light to dark. Headlights on, I continued.

Minutes passed and then, without warning, the bike lost all power and I slowed to a stop. I suspected a blocked fuel filter. If that were the case, it wasn't the first time and there was no way to fix it at the roadside. By my estimate, I was about four miles out from the Hall.

With the rain now breaking through the canopy, bike parked and secured at the side of the road, shopping bag in one hand, helmet in the other, I began the walk home.

Among the noise of boughs creaking and rain falling through leaves, there came the distinct sound of hooves and once again, out of the gloom, came a horse and rider. I recognized Maximus and his stallion immediately and stepped to the side of the narrow lane to let them pass. Water dripped down my face, my newly blown-dried and bouncing hair now sodden and clinging to my face.

"Whoa!"

Despite my efforts, the horse reared and once again I was trapped beneath its hooves. My reaction was instant and instinctive. I flung out my arms in a wide and defensive sweep. Powerful energy flowed from my shoulders and out through my palms creating a translucent barrier of iridescent sparks. The moment became static—Maximus rearing with the horse.

Our eyes locked. His were topaz ringed with black, the iris glittering. It was the moment from my dream! I hadn't relived the moment in the lane, I had foreseen it, dreamt of this moment. With the horse held back by magick, an iridescent shield between us, I stepped out from beneath its hooves. Safely away from the beast, the spell broke.

"What the devil!"

Again, the horse reared, snorting and pulling against the reins as Maximus struggled to control it. "Down, you devil! Down!"

Maximus guided the horse to the other side of the lane, calming the beast into submission before dismounting. Brows tightly knit, he cast me a thunderous glance. From the distance, as if matching his mood, came the rumble of thunder. Rain spattered my head, the canopy, now drenched, offered little protection from the downpour.

"What the devil are you doing?" he growled.

He was blaming me again, but I was in no mood to be made to feel stupid. After thirty years of being blamed for everything from burnt toast to lost suits to failing libidos I said 'No!' to that toxic message.

"It is not my fault that you can't control your horse."

"What?" He towered above me. "Are you blaming me, witch?"

Witch? Until that moment I had denied being a witch. Even when my hands had sparked in the garden I had resisted. Since childhood, being called a witch was a word other people had used against me, had thrown at me to cause me pain, to 'other' me and create division and ridicule. But now I realized it was because they saw me as a threat. Now, I embraced it. "Yes," I replied, "I am. You could have killed me."

His eyes glittered, just as Aelfwen's had, but where hers held the promise of magick, Maximus' held the threat of something far darker. Did mine glitter too?

Disbelief stared back at me. "You were in the middle of the road."

"It's a narrow lane. And I was walking as close to the wall as I could. You were galloping in the middle of the lane – again! You nearly ran me down!"

"I was riding my horse!"

"You were galloping ... in the dark."

"Pah! It is not nighttime!"

"Perhaps you should have lights on a helmet or wear a hi-vis vest? Then you would be able to see where you're going."

The sun broke through the clouds and light filtered through the canopy. Maximus was as sodden as me and I couldn't help but notice the wet shirt now clinging to his muscular chest. He remained close, towering over me.

"You startled my horse, witch! Aelfwen said that you had been cleansed. You must be more toxic than she thought."

What? "How dare you! I am not toxic."

"The horse senses it."

That couldn't be. Only this morning I had visited the stable and fed it a carrot from the bucket outside its door. There had been no sign of it reacting to me badly. "I am not toxic" I repeated. "And I'll prove it."

"I accept that challenge. Go ahead," he gestured to Cosimo with a sweep of his arm. "Prove it."

"Right! I will." Doubt began to weasel its way into my thoughts but before it had a chance to take hold, I walked across the narrow lane to Cosimo. The stallion raised its head and snorted as I approached but remained still. He eyed me with one huge brown eye, snorted once more as though to greet me then quieted. With a gentle touch, I stroked his mane, then the side of his nose. He showed no signs of anxiety, in fact, he was completely calm. "Hah!" I exclaimed. "See! I am not the poisonous one."

Maximus grunted but made no effort at apologizing. Instead, he strode over to us and took hold of the rein. The horse nickered and shifted, the calm evaporating and pulled against his master. "It's you!" I said as I watched the horse change. "It's you he's reacting to."

"Nonsense. This horse knows me well. Why would he react to me?"

Perhaps you're toxic? I didn't voice my thoughts Maximus was my boss after all and I'd already pushed my defiance to the limit. A sinking sensation washed over me. Maximus was my boss! My heart sank with the realization that I had offended the man who employed me. I'd blown it. He wouldn't want me working for him after this!

Despair began to seep back in. I'd messed up – again. Gerald's voice echoed. 'You ruin everything, Leofe! You always do.'

As Maximus spoke soothing words to the horse, it stopped resisting and grew calm.

"What are you doing here? You're miles from the Hall."

"My bike, it broke down. I've been into town." I didn't elaborate and explaining to this man that I'd been to have my hair done, my eyebrows shaped, and my facial hair obliterated because I looked like a frump compared to his girlfriend wasn't something I realized fully.

"Your hair's shorter." He said with bluntness whilst scrutinizing my face. "And you have makeup on. Well, you had it on, the rain has made it run down your face."

"I had a haircut." My tone was more defensive than I intended.

"You're wet."

"It's raining."

He continued to stare.

"Anyway," I said growing uncomfortable under his scrutiny. "I'd better get back." My plans were to call for a tow company to pick up my bike. I had no money to repair it so would have to sell it or garage it until I had saved up enough money. After organizing it for collection, I'd start looking for another job. From the way Maximus was looking at me I had little doubt our next meeting would be to terminate our contract. What contract? I hadn't signed anything, so they didn't even need to do that. I kept my disheartened sigh to myself and began the long walk back to the Hall. Maximus grunted as he mounted the horse. I picked up my steps; I didn't want him to see the misery I was beginning to feel. Hooves struck against the road and then he was beside me.

"Get on," he demanded.

I continued walking. "No, it's alright. I can walk."

"You can ride with me."

"No, I'm fine," I insisted.

He muttered something unintelligible. "Witch!"

"Yes?"

"You are being stubborn."

"I'm just walking."

He pulled on the reins. The horse slowed and he dismounted.

"You're wet. There are many miles to walk, and the rain is coming."

"I'm fine and anyway, the sun is out."

Thunder rumbled as if to prove me wrong and the leaves rustled, whipped by the wind.

"A storm is coming."

Once again, heavy grey clouds slid across the sun and the lane grew gloomy. Wind whistled through the trees.

"Ride with me."

As rain began to spatter and another roll of thunder vibrated through the air, I relented.

"Do you ride?" he asked.

"Not horses," I replied.

"Then let me show you. It's easy."

The horse was enormous and getting up into the saddle looked impossible.

"Just put your foot in the stirrup, grab the saddle and pull yourself up."

The stirrup was almost at waist height. "I don't think I can manage that."

He grunted and then, without warning, his arms circled my waist and he held me tight against his chest, effortlessly lifting me off the ground. His beard bristled against my cheek.

"What are you doing? Put me down!"

"Put your foot in the stirrup," he grunted taking a step towards the horse.

I slipped my boot into the stirrup.

"Good, now swing your leg over the saddle."

This part I could do. I grabbed the pommel of the saddle but before I had a chance to lift my leg, Maximus placed a large hand on my buttock and pushed. I lurched forward, face close to the horse's mane as Maximus grabbed my thigh, parted my legs, and set me down on the saddle.

"There!" he said with triumph. "You're on."

I managed a grunted 'thanks' and had barely recovered before he mounted the horse and sat behind me. Huge arms slipped around my waist, and I was in his grip, my back tight against his belly and chest. Breath caught in my throat as my body reacted to his touch. I was aware of every inch of his body against mine as the horse began to walk and we moved in rhythm together. Gerald's neglect had forced my libido into hibernation, but now my body began to wake from the sleep it had resigned itself to.

Don't go there, Leofe. He's your boss! He's arrogant. Full of himself and he has a girlfriend. He'd never look at you. You're a fool to even think he would.

Each passing minute was exquisite torture as my body betrayed me. I wanted this man. I hated wanting this man. I was a stupid fool. He would dismiss any idea of being interested in me with the bat of an eyelid and a bemused, incredulous laugh.

We arrived at Blackwood Hall to intense thunder, torrential rain and Marissa leaving. She slowed in her sleek and bright red car to allow us to pass and watched slack-jawed and confused. Breath steamed the car window as her eyes narrowed to a scowl and I imagined her jealous energy filling the car like a toxic green gas. Maximus merely raised a hand to thank her for letting us pass. I doubted he had even noticed her ugly scowl.

In the courtyard Maximus dismounted. Lightheaded and still overwhelmed by the intensity of my desire for him, I mumbled thanks as he helped me down, made a lame joke about being wet then practically ran back to my apartment, slamming the door tightly shut behind me. Water formed a pool around my boots as I gathered my senses, shocked that I could feel this way after such a long time. Despite being lonely, I had surrendered to the fact that I would be single forevermore, that men were more trouble than they were worth, and that, at fifty-one, my days of 'romance', and even needing a man for 'that' were over. I had been wrong, so very, very wrong.

After showering, and in a desperate effort to distract my thoughts, I spent the rest of the afternoon organizing the collection of my bike from the lane.

Chapter Twenty-Two

The remainder of the weekend passed without drama, and I turned up for work on Monday fully expecting to be fired that day but forced myself to push that fear to the back of my mind.

As I snipped another handful of brown stems from last year's foxgloves, I stood back to admire my work. The morning had been glorious with the rolling mist burned off by the late May sun. Birds chittered in the trees and hedges, and I had even seen a wren, may favourite bird, perched among the ivy that wound itself between the garden's iron fence. Hidden by years of growth, the fence formed a large circle around the garden and had become a paradise of tangled branches and vines perfect for raising a family. The tangle of hawthorn, ivy, and briars would have to be trimmed back at the end of the nesting season, but I would make sure it was done with care (if I was still here). The branches would not be hacked and mutilated on my watch.

As I stretched my back, surveying the now tidy bed, I became aware of a tingling sensation at the back of my neck—I was being watched.

I turned to a large pair of sunglasses, a mass of bleached blonde hair, and a sour pout, stained bright pink.

"Marissa! I didn't realise you were there."

I had been so engrossed in tending to the poisonous plants that I hadn't heard her heels crunching across the gravel. She continued to point, staring at me from behind her glasses with narrowed eyes. My guess was that she thought the dark lenses hid her scowl, unless she was brazen enough to give me a filthy look to my face.

"I saw you the other day."

So, we're dispensing with the pleasantries. "Oh? What day was that?" I asked although I knew exactly which day she meant.

"On Saturday. You were with Maximus. On his horse."

"Oh, yeah! My bike broke down in the lane. He gave me a lift – well, a ride – back." I laughed as though it were no big deal and hadn't completely derailed me.

"I bet he did," she smirked.

Her lips puckered. I could see that she was seething with jealousy. I decided to tweak her. I dropped the handful of cuttings into the waiting bucket. "You know, I've never ridden a horse but, with Maximus so close behind me, and his arm around my waist, I felt," I eyed her, "safe."

Her lips thinned and she removed her sunglasses. "Lucky you!" she laughed, then said, "I just wondered if you'd like to join me one evening for drinks." The brow had uncreased, the thinned lips were now full. "There's a great cocktail bar in town. I was in there last week with one of the girls. It was heaving. Lots of older single men too, out on the prowl. Or younger—if that's more your thing. You'd love it."

I didn't like the way she said I'd 'love it' but perhaps I'd misjudged her and, given I was yet to meet anyone to just have fun girls' nights out with, I accepted. "Sure, sounds fun. It's been a while."

"I can tell," she said whilst arching a brow, "but I like your new hairdo." She gestured to my hair. "Did you go to

Sylvester's? They're great and can make a silk purse out of any old sow. So talented!"

I couldn't make Marissa out. On the one hand she dripped scorn onto me and on the other she wanted us to go out for a 'fun' evening. I suspected ulterior motives but decided to rise to the challenge and give as good as I got. "So," I smiled. "Do *you* go there?"

She laughed, recognizing the comeback and, despite the smile, her eyes narrowed behind the lenses of her sunglasses. "No," she stated. "I go to Angelo's. Quite exclusive. Angelo charges an obscene amount, but so worth it. Anyway, Thursday at eight. I'll meet you at The First Wives Club. I know hilarious name for a bar, and its heaving with old cougars, but it does draw in the meat." She cackled. "I thought you'd like it."

Suddenly, I was far less enthusiastic about going to that particular bar and definitely not interested in picking up younger men, even if, at fifty-one, I fitted into the 'cougar' category.

"Ask for the afternoon off. We can go into town and check out the boutique—buy you something with a bit of sparkle. She looked me up and down. Something with a plunging neckline so you can show a bit of cleavage." Her eyes were locked to mine. She was enjoying herself. "Unless of course you'd rather not? I mean, older women do get a bit crepey across the décolletage, particularly if they've enjoyed a lot of sun." She glanced to the sky and then back at me, her meaning obvious – I was a gardener and spent much of my day enjoying a 'lot of sun'.

"No, I'm fine with a plunging neckline," I replied.

She laughed. "Wonderful. It's a date then. Tell Aelfwen you're taking Thursday afternoon off. I'll clear it with Max."

Refusing would be impolite. I nodded. "Okay," I replied with a sinking sensation. "It'll be fun."

"Good. I'm sure that we'll have a great time."

"I'm sure we will."

"And become great friends."

She was totally disingenuous and either didn't care that I could see through her fakery or was a terrible actress—maybe both.

She turned to walk away then swung back round. "And I'll tell you all about Maximus. They do say he's married."

"Married?"

"Yes, didn't you know?"

"He's my boss," I replied. "It's none of my business."

She laughed. "And that's not the worst thing. They say he keeps her locked up." She glanced at the house and jabbed a highly polished nail at the roof. "In there. In the attic."

Without waiting for my response, she strode away.

I remembered the noises I'd heard in the night. The mysterious woman who had come from the attic rooms, the woman no one had introduced me to.

It was like something out of the plot of a novel – a secluded gothic mansion, a darkly brooding owner, a wife locked in the attic! It was! Jane Eyre by Charlotte Bronte. Maximus was Rochester. I was Jane! And the strange noises I'd heard coming from the attic were the crazy wife he'd been tricked into marrying and locked away. It would explain the mysterious woman I'd seen that no one had introduced me to. She must be the mental health nurse assigned to the wife. It was a modern-day Gothic novel. And how did that end? I sighed. If only. 'Reader, I married him!'

I stood in stunned silence and then laughed aloud. Marissa was obviously trying to cause trouble. "Stupid woman!" It was nonsense. It had to be. There would be a rational explanation for it all. The attics were no doubt now suites like mine and used to house members of staff, not crazed wives.

Chapter Twenty-Three

Nagging doubts continued to dog me but the following morning, with the sun already promising another warm day, I relegated thoughts of the attic and who might be up there to the back of my mind and instead focused on organizing a major project. I was itching to tidy the topiary and water feature at the front of the house, but my job this morning, I had decided, was to tackle the courtyard knot garden; a beautiful space created from box hedging laid out in an intricate geometric design that would be a great draw for visitors. The previous evening, I had begun to do some research on other grand houses with gardens open to the public. Most of them had attractive and easily navigable websites that included a ticket booking facility. Blackwood Hall did not, and this was an issue I was going to suggest that we consider at the next meeting.

Surrounded by walls clad with ivy and rambling roses, with wide beds filled with flowers, and thousands of box plants forming the intricate knots, the garden needed constant attention to keep it in pristine shape. Like the rest of the gardens at the Hall, it had been neglected and left to become unruly. Determined to return it to its former glory, I began to make a list of jobs that needed doing and had asked Aldred and Drew to meet me after lunch for their input. There was an enormous amount of work to be done and it was obvious from the overgrown state of many of the garden areas, that the men needed guidance, or at least a gentle prod to get them to put in the effort once more. It had been a while since I'd managed a team of gardeners, but it had been a good experience and I was hopeful that the men would accept me without too many problems.

I stepped closer to the knot. With its intricately woven pattern, it was a work of art.

"It's based on the fabric of the dress my mother wore when she was presented at court."

I turned to face Maximus. "You startled me! I didn't hear you. It's beautiful. The dress must have been stunning."

"It was." He gestured towards the house. "There's a painting of her wearing it in the long gallery. If you'd like to see the original ... We have it stored, somewhere."

"I'd love to." Seeing the original dress from which the garden had been designed would be amazing.

He smiled. "I appreciate your enthusiasm. It's refreshing. She sat for Hans Holbein."

I could only stare at him as my mind made efforts to process his words. Hans Holbein had painted Henry VIII, the Tudor king. There was no way that he could have painted Maximus' mother. "Hans Holbein the Younger?" *But that's not possible!*

He nodded. "The very same. Towards the end of his life, apparently. It was finished not long before he died of plague, in London."

"I had no idea he died of the plague."

"It was rife back then."

He had to be pulling my leg. "Back when exactly?"

"When Henry was on the throne."

I realized he was watching for my response, a mirthful glint in his eyes. "And your mother was alive then?" I asked. He nodded. "So, I guess that makes you ancient too," I threw back.

He raised a brow then laughed. "I guess it does. So, you were very focused when I startled you." He gestured to my clipboard where I had made copious notes. "Taking your job seriously?"

"Yes." I held up the clipboard for him to see. "I'm making a list of everything that needs to be done in this garden."

"Are you planning on doing it all yourself?"

"No. I'm meeting the other gardeners later to discuss it."

He nodded his approval.

"It's a beautiful garden," I said to fill the silence.

"It is," he agreed. "Leofe, come with me. I want to show you around."

"Now?"

"Yes, now."

Without waiting for my response, he began to walk away.

I followed, forced to quicken my step to keep up.

He remained silent as we walked, making no effort at small talk, and led me to a yard of brick outbuildings and a stone barn that faced the area of open grass and the vast forest beyond that. The double doors to the barn were open. Inside was a tractor and numerous tools and farming implements hung on hooks but at the entrance was a quadbike. Maximus strode over to the quad and seated himself upon it.

"Come on. You can sit behind me."

Taken by surprise, I stalled. My body would be pressed to his! I would feel the strength of his body against mine! "I-"

"What's wrong?" he asked. "You'll be safe." He offered me a wry smile. "It's not a horse."

"I'm not scared!" I said. *I'm terrified! Terrified of being so close to you again. You already fill my dreams!* "I've ridden one before."

The last thing I wanted to do was sit behind him on the quad. Every part of me railed against the growing attraction I had for this man. I had put the need to love and be loved to bed once. I could do it again.

"I thought you'd enjoy seeing around the estate. I know you ride a motorbike, so I thought this would be fun."

You can do this, Leofe. He's your boss. Be professional. Again, I stalled. Riding on horseback with him had been overwhelming. I felt a familiar tingle in my fingers and heard a crackle like an electrical spark. I gripped the clipboard to my chest and stuffed the tingling hand in my jeans pocket.

"So, it's just me that your worried about?"

Yes! I think I may spontaneously combust! "No. I'm sure you're capable-"

"So, get on then."

Just get on, Leofe. "Right," I said. "I will."

He laughed and as he held my gaze the topaz of his eyes glittered. My heart beat hard, I watched his full lips move without hearing the words. Placing my hands on his shoulders, willing my fingers to remain spark free, I swung my leg over the seat. As I slid down behind him, the engine thrummed into life.

"Put your arms around my waist," he shouted over the noise.

"I'm okay."

"You sure?"

"Sure."

"Hold on tight!"

The quad began to move with a jerk, and I was thrown backwards then forwards.

Instinctively, I wrapped my arms around Maximus' waist and locked my tingling fingers. He flinched and grew tense but opened up the throttle and steered the quadbike out of the yard. Certain that I had electrocuted him with my nervous energy, I willed myself to become calm. Being so close to him would intoxicate me if I let my defenses down and I was determined not to let that happen. I took a calming breath and focused on the scenery.

"I wanted to show you round the estate," he shouted over his shoulder as we left the yard and joined a narrow road that cut between the fields. Either side of us cows chewed the cud, several with calves. "This herd belongs to McNair. He's one of our longest standing tenant farmers. His family have kept their herds here for generations," he explained as we passed another field of cows.

We continued along the road, passing numerous fields. Some held flocks of sheep with their lambs, others more cows, and one had several llamas and a number of goats. In the far distance I spotted several deer with their offspring.

As we moved further away from the house, Maximus seemed to relax, the tension easing from his body. The road diverged and he took the route towards the woodlands. Shaded and cool, the trees were a welcome relief from the increasingly hot sun, and we continued along the road for several minutes before turning off onto a track. The land began to rise in a gentle slope and Maximus slowed the bike to a stop.

"We walk from here," he said and waited for me to dismount. "Shall we?" He gestured to the rising hill.

I was alone in the woodlands with a man who exuded danger that I knew very little about and who was suspected of having locked his crazy wife in the attic. "Where are we going?" I asked, hanging back as he took several steps forward.

He turned, surprised that I hadn't followed him. "I won't bite."

I stood without moving, uncertain.

He frowned. "Honestly, I won't bite. I get it. Listen, there's something I want you to see. It's just over the hill. Follow me." He turned and took large steps up the steep incline then disappeared over the brow.

I was being absurd. I followed him, running up the bank. In the distance was a small clearing and at its centre a mound. Beyond that I noticed a small cottage.

"Are we going to the cottage?" I asked, intrigued by the woodland home.

"No. That's Wyman's cottage, our woodland manager."

I remembered that Jodi had mentioned him, made a joke of him being single and available.

"I wanted you to see the barrow." He pointed to the grass covered mound in the clearing. Circled by trees, it rose from the ground with gentle slopes.

"The hill?"

"It's a burial mound. Come, let us visit." Without waiting for me, he strode ahead and once again I was left to catch up.

We made our way through the trees and stood at the edge of the mound. Oval in shape, it rose with gentle slopes to shoulder height.

"Who's buried here?"

"A thegn and his wife. They were murdered by a local chieftain, but they were much loved and given a royal burial."

"Does someone tend it?" I asked. "I'm surprised that the trees haven't grown around it."

"Wyman tends the area, but trees don't grow here. Their grave is protected. Torsten and his wife Astrid were the first Guardians. When our people settled here, in the earliest days, they grew aware of the nature of this place. Revna, a seer, one of our great vardlokkurs, foresaw their deaths. Sometimes, I come here just to sit with them. Sometimes, they sit with me."

"You sit with their ghosts?" A chill ran through me.

He nodded. "If that's what you call their spirit, then yes. Did you know that the Sutton Hoo treasure was discovered because the landowner noticed spirits walking near the barrow?"

I shook my head. "No. I had no idea."

"It's true. The archaeologists found incredible treasure but destroyed the barrow too. That will never happen here. It is our duty to protect the barrow. We have protected it for more than a thousand years. We claimed the land, expanded it, and it has been safe, but in this age, the space between the barrow and the outside world is shrinking. Much of the land beyond ours has been cultivated and now that land is being sold for construction. At the very edge of Blackwood land, on the eastern boundary, is an industrial estate. Beside that, also along our boundary, a vast tract of arable land has been sold for building and a new estate of nearly one thousand homes is planned. The world seems to be shrinking, Leofe."

"It is," I agreed, remembering the huge estate that had been built on farmland where Gerald and Cordelia lived. An effort had been made by local people and environmentalists to stop it going ahead. "But they can't build on Blackwood land unless you sell it."

"Which I never will."

"Good. It's too special to lose."

He turned to me with a smile. "Now that is a refreshing attitude. I cannot tell you how difficult it is to find someone who understands. They're all for what they call 'progress' and turning land into carparks, out of town shopping malls, or housing.'

"Or theme parks."

He laughed. "Yes, or theme parks."

"You don't think Marissa's idea is a good one then?"

"Hell no!" He sighed and cast his gaze back to the barrow. "But we must make money somehow. This place cannot be kept in good repair through magick alone. It is far too big. The energy it takes ..."

I sensed his exhaustion.

"I'll help where I can," I offered, although I felt out of my depth. "But marketing isn't my thing."

He smiled, catching my eyes. "What is your thing, Leofe? What makes you tick?"

"I ... I'm not sure, I guess. I've been wrapped up for so long in such ... well, stuck in a bad marriage, that I haven't given it much thought."

"I know what that feels like," he said. "I was married too, once, long ago—a lifetime ago."

"Was it a mistake? Your marriage?"

He nodded. "A painful mistake."

"Mine was ... Looking back, I'm not sure why I even married Gerald."

"To fit in. To be like them."

"You may be right. It's what all my friends were doing."

"You never fit in at school, or college, but you learned how to behave, to be like them."

"How did you know?"

"It's something most of us have had to do. The world senses our difference. Rejects us until we learn how to become like them."

"Fake it to make it," I said.

He laughed, catching my eyes. His glittered topaz and held mine. "Yes, fake it to make it."

"I can be myself here," I stated the words tumbling out. "I love it here. The garden, being among the flowers, gives me peace."

"You nurture the earth," he stated.

"I want to help. I want to heal what Man has damaged, yes."

He nodded. "You are welcome here, Leofe."

"You've all made me so welcome. It's the first time I've felt that I fit in—anywhere."

"Living among humans does that to us. We don't fit in because we are different, and they sense that. And when they grow to fear us ... that is when the hunting begins." He glanced back at the barrow. "Man has a need to weed out those who don't conform to their rules and destroy them."

I remembered Barry's face when I spotted him up the ladder. He had seen me touch the fronds of the fern and destroy them with a simple touch. He had heard my hex before falling off the ladder and fear made him spiteful. "Man can certainly be cruel," I agreed.

From the cottage a man waved. Maximus returned the wave then turned to me.

"Wyman?"

"Yes. I shall visit him later. Now," he said turning to me, "I've taken up too much of your time. I know that you have much work to do."

I didn't want to leave. The warmth of the afternoon sun, standing close to Maximus, sharing our innermost thoughts, had been a perfect moment. I felt welcome and appreciated. I felt as though I had been accepted and was part of something special. I felt that I mattered to him, that he appreciated me, that he wouldn't abuse my trust or belittle me in the way that Gerald had, for decades. "Come on," he smiled. "Aelfwen will give me a telling off if I keep you too long, and Jodi will accuse me of 'liking' you."

I laughed. "She accuses me of the same."

He held my gaze, then laughed as he gestured to the quad-bike. "Let's go home."

Chapter Twenty-Four

Thursday afternoon arrived and I met Marissa in town as arranged. Despite my misgivings, and her earlier cattiness, I had a surprisingly enjoyable afternoon. Any hint of jealousy seemed to have evaporated. We visited her favourite boutiques and she picked out various outfits that she thought I'd look good in. Some revealed a little more flesh than I was prepared to show and eventually I bought a new pair of slim-fitting white jeans and a silky blouse with Japanese inspired prints of peonies. It was beautiful and something I'd never have ordinarily bought, but Marissa persuaded me. "You're worth it, darling. Treat yourself! You've landed a fabulous new job. It's your reward for all your hard work and ... all the troubles you've had to endure."

What did she know about my 'troubles' Marissa's words were vague enough to be a generalization – didn't we all have 'troubles'? – and I didn't want to 'out' myself by asking what she knew. Blackwood Hall was a new start. No one knew about my past. No one here knew about Gerald and his bigamous marriage, or how he'd chosen a fat blonde over me, his loving and faithful wife of thirty years, and had two kids with her whilst I suspected absolutely nothing!

You suspected, Leofe. You just chose to close your eyes to the truth.

Despite her words, there was no hint of any effort to hurt me. Quite the opposite, Marissa was kind and friendly without fault that afternoon. I had a good time. We stopped for coffee and cakes at her favourite café then shopped for lipstick and agreed that I would borrow a pair of her heels – 'simply gorgeous strappy gold sandals' – that would go 'perfectly' with my new white jeans. She would have them delivered to the Hall by taxi and I could return in that taxi and meet her at The First Wives Club.

"You are going to look fabulous, darling and we are going to have such fun!"

If she was being disingenuous, I couldn't tell. With an air kiss either side of my cheeks, we said our goodbyes and I returned by taxi to the Hall, all dread at the thought of an evening with Marissa 'mega-bitch' Lewis gone. Tonight was going to be fun. And Marissa was right, after what I'd been through, I deserved a little fun. I'd avoid the younger men though—being a 'cougar' was definitely not my thing.

The taxi arrived at 7.30 pm, complete with gold and strappy sandals as promised. Marissa was right; they did look great with the new jeans. I'd lost weight, had a tan, and with my new hairdo felt and looked better than I had in years. I was ready to hit the town. "You scrub up well, even if I do say so myself," I smiled at my reflection, admiring how flattering the jeans and sandals were. "Not too shabby for fifty-one."

'The First Wives Club' was tucked away down a narrow street in the centre of town. The bar was double fronted with large multi-paned bow windows either side of a heavy, half-glass door. There was no sign of Marissa outside, so I went inside. The place was heaving, just as Marissa had promised. The bar had been converted from what had probably been a shop, but several walls had been knocked out to join several rooms together making it long and narrow.

Seating areas flanked the first area where there had once been shelves of produce and a till, whilst in the next there was a bar to the left and a narrow area for seating opposite backed by a raised floor filled with tables. People thronged around the bar as a singer stood in an alcove, acoustic guitar in hand, sipping from a pint of beer.

I scanned the room, looking for Marissa in the sea of people. Standing there alone, watching everyone else talk and laugh in groups, I felt out of place, self-conscious and my old uncertainty began to prod.

"Leofe!"

"Marissa!" Relief.

Marissa was suddenly at my side, and I was in the fold once again—one of them.

"You look amazing, darling. Come on, let's get some drinks."

She grabbed my hand and pulled me forward leading the way, weaving through the throngs of people. As promised, there were plenty of men and I was relieved to see that most were at least thirty and that, despite its name, the bar attracted plenty of much younger women too. It wasn't quite the cougarville Marissa had painted it to be.

The singer mumbled something into the mic that I couldn't decipher above the clamour of voices and began to strum his guitar then launched into an acoustic rendition of Radiohead's 'Creep'.

"See, I told you it would be heaving!"

I nodded. "Great atmosphere!"

The bar tender mixed cocktails as another took an order and another squeezed a slice of lime over ice cubes.

"What do you want to drink?" she asked. Then, without waiting for an answer shouted, "Porn Stars!"

"What?"

She turned from me and ordered the drinks. There was little point in trying to speak. I waited, took my drink when it was placed on the bar, then followed her up the steps and onto the raised area. Hips swaying as she walked, she headed straight for a table in the corner. It was already occupied by a couple of guys, but they were happy to share. I was relieved to sit down and get out of the bustle. Chatter and laughter filled the place and Marissa took a sip of her 'Porn Star' cocktail and passed me a shot glass.

I hadn't led a completely secluded life, even if it had been a bit lonely with Gerald so often at 'work' aka living with his secret family, but this was the first cocktail bar I'd been to. The cocktail tasted sweet, like fruit juice, and was easy to drink. Clear liquid filled the shot glass. "What is it?"

"Prosecco," Marissa shouted above the noise, "to go with your cocktail."

She lifted her own shot glass and downed it, then watched as I downed mine, her smile broad. It tasted bitter and I remembered why I wasn't keen on Prosecco.

"So, ladies, do you come here often?"

Marissa laughed and brushed her manicured and polished nails across the back of the man's hand in a provocative way. A large and bearded man with a huge belly guffawed and her reply was lost in the noise. Marissa seemed cheap and sleezy, but the men enjoyed her attention. Both were at least twenty years younger than me. I gauged that Marissa had to be around forty, so they were a good deal younger than her too. Before I'd had a chance to take the last sip of my cocktail another arrived, courtesy of our companions. Marissa slipped beside the more handsome of the two, whispering into his ear. From his smile I knew it was something suggestive. His hand stroked her knee. I took a sip of the new cocktail. It tasted sweet but had a bitter aftertaste. My head began to throb, and my heartbeat speed up. Voices waxed and waned. I was suddenly light-headed.

"Leofe!" Marissa's voice seemed distant as though spoken through cloth. "Leofe!"

The bar and the heaving mass of people closed in on me. Their bodies flexed as though printed on fabric blown by the wind. I tried to stand but was dragged back down. Marissa's laughing face was huge before me. The men's frowning faces loomed. I was lifted. The sound of laughter was overwhelming.

The bar grew dark, and the throng of men and women disappeared. All became silent.

Blackness pervaded.

My ears rang with a high-pitched wheedling tone.

"Leofe!"

From the distance came men's voices. Within me were other voices. 'Don't speak. Remain silent. Keep your secrets'.

Pain shot through my upper arm and then my thigh as though I had been thumped or kicked. I groaned. Bright light shone into my face. I tried to shield my eyes, but my arms felt numb, paralysed.

Voices filled my ears and my head.

Voices that mingled. Questioning and demanding. Telling me to speak. Telling me to stay silent.

There was a smell too—acrid, pungent, fresh, chemical.

My head throbbed but when I tried to lift it and look, the bright lights blinded me. I could see nothing of the room.

"She knows nothing," I heard a woman speak. Marissa?

"Marissa," I called. "Help!"

"She's coming round."

As the minutes passed, I realized I was laying on a bed. Heels tapped across the floor and sunlight flooded the room.

"You're awake! Good." Marissa's voice was saccharine sweet. "Your taxi is outside."

Still barely conscious, Marissa helped me to my feet and led me to the front door of her apartment. There a man, tall with a dark beard, took me by the arm and helped me down the stairs and into the waiting taxi.

The journey back home was a blur of rushing fields and trees, nausea and debilitating headache. Light made the pain in my head and the nausea worse. Everything was bathed in strange colours. I closed my eyes and endured the swerving of the car as it wound round the narrow and winding lanes. Gravel crunched and I opened my eyes to Blackwood Hall. The man opened the passenger door. I fumbled in my bag for my purse.

"No need. Prepaid."

"Thanks," I managed.

He tutted. "Drinking no good," he said. "My adwise – you no drink no more. Is dangerous for women."

My head throbbed. The memories of last night were confused and empty, blank after the shot of Prosecco. "I didn't—migraine."

"Okay, lady. As you like. I give adwise. Is not my business. But if you my wife I would not allow."

"Thanks!" I mumbled. He returned to his car, and I returned to my apartment, head pounding, nausea swelling, desperate to reach the safety of my room before anyone saw me.

What the hell happened last night?

My mobile began to ring just as the apartment door closed with a thud behind me.

"Hello?"

"Just checking you got home okay." Marissa.

"I- Yeah."

Tinkling laugh. "I didn't realise you drank so much, darling."

"I don't!" Head pounding.

"I couldn't keep up with you. I bet your feet are killing you, but you made the boys very, very happy." Again, the deriding laugh. It was horrible.

"Boys? Happy?"

"It was fun. We must do it again."

"What happened? I can't remember."

There was no answer. The phone was dead.

A wave of nausea hit, and I ran to the bathroom, hanging my head over the toilet only just in time. What had happened? Had I ...

Had they ...

Nothing had happened. It couldn't have. I felt sure of that. I would know if I had done *that* ... wouldn't I? I retched, vomited into the toilet bowl then slid to the floor. "Poison," I whispered. "I've been poisoned."

Chapter Twenty-Five

Friday morning passed in a blur of sleeping but when I eventually roused enough to remain conscious, my thirst for water was unquenchable. After a fifth glass my need slowed and I staggered to the bathroom, took a hot shower, then curled up on the bed. I felt violated but could not believe that what Marissa had alluded to - that I'd slept with those men - had actually happened.

Something had happened though. There was no way that one cocktail could render me blacked out. My drink had been spiked. It had to have been, but what had taken place during the hours between me drinking the spiked cocktail and being bundled into the taxi was a haze of jumbled images and noises, none of which made sense. Questions repeated, spoken by unknown voices. There were figures without faces, and a wall of colourful images, photographs of a house, gardens, people, horses, close-ups of windows, maps, torn pages filled with writing and symbols. 'Ask him what's in the attic', 'Where is he keeping the key?' 'You made them very, very happy'. Lights, cameras, a tripod, candles. Sweat beaded my forehead. Cameras? A tripod? I curled into a tight ball, cringeing at the repeated phrase, 'very, very happy' but by mid-afternoon I had recovered enough to make myself a slice of toast. Twice someone knocked at the door. The first was Jodi and later Aelfwen. I ignored them both with no idea how I would explain my absence. No doubt they would guess I had a hangover or perhaps Marissa would tell them?

After two rounds of toast, I felt a little better. The nausea had abated, and I was left with overwhelming fatigue and a sense of weakness. A dull ache still sat at the base of my skull but the painful tension across the front of my brow and in my eyes had gone. The colour of things was back to normal. That I had been drugged I was in no doubt, but to what purpose I could not bring myself to consider.

"Never again," I whispered. "Never. Again."

As evening approached, the room grew chill, and I lit the fire. The glow and warmth were soothing, and I sat on the sofa, legs tucked to the side and opened my mother's grimoire. Words shifted on the page, and I closed my eyes, pinching the bridge of my nose then tried again. I hadn't noticed how beautiful the book was before today and switched on the lamp to take a closer look as the sun began to sink. Orange light filled the room, spilling across my lap and the open book. The air around it shimmered as particles of dust caught in the sun's still warm rays and eddied. Each page was filled with recipes, symbols, and instructions. I read through many peculiar charms, spells, and recipes: 'A charme for the dropsy', 'A goode spelle for dyscovering of the truthe', 'Howe to skin a frog so that it sufficeth'. Some made me curious: 'Howe to stop a manne that shalle be hanged', and 'Howe to make fire burnethe colde'. If my mother had written them down, then she must have done so for good reason. Had she ever used them?

The pages of the book weren't made of paper, and I had a vague knowledge that years ago, hundreds of years ago, books were made of animal skins. The pages of my mother's book were yellow and stiff with age. Some were thicker than others and more than one had a misshapen hole, some retained hair and were dotted with what could have been evidence of follicles.

"How old are you?"

The cover was made of leather and into the border was carved a simple pattern. There was nothing fancy about it – no gold corner decorations, no gold edging, or metal clasp to lock it. Instead, a thick leather thong, well-worn and repaired, was used to tie it together. At the back were bundles of loose pages. It had the air of a book well used, a workhorse. The last entry was a date – the day I was born.

"You stopped then, didn't you." I placed a finger beside the entry, remembering my mother – the warmth of her embrace, those amazing eyes. You knew you were in trouble when the iris grew dark. They sparkled when she laughed, and we had laughed a lot.

At the front of the book the pages, at least a quarter of the entire volume, were written in a runic script. Later pages were in cursive but a language I didn't recognize, the pages closest to the end were the ones I could read most easily and though they seemed to be spelled erratically and without following the modern 'rules', I guessed that these must have been my mother's contribution.

"How old are you?" I repeated.

The evening wore on and I chose a few of the recipes that I thought might be useful and placed a marker to keep my place. My head swam with possibilities. If I was a witch, I wanted to know how to use my powers and then I would be protected and never allow myself to be abused as I had last night. Could I use them to get revenge?

The night wore on and I watched the flickering fire, too tired to continue reading. I considered watching a film but could find nothing to interest me on the television so switched it off and sat before the orange glow, allowing myself to sink back into sleep; tomorrow would be another day. I was safe. Nothing could hurt me here. Marissa's cackling face floated into my memory, but I pushed it away. "Tomorrow," I murmured. "I'll sort it tomorrow."

I woke to a woman shouting and the banging of a door. It came from upstairs—in the attic.

'Ask him!'

'Ask him what's in the attic.'

"Ask him what he keeps up there.'

This time, I determined to discover exactly what the source of the noise was and put Marissa's suspicions to rest or confirm them!

Night had fallen and the hallways sat in grey shadow as I made my way up several flights of stairs and followed the noise.

"This time," I whispered, "I'm going to find out. What are you hiding up here, Maximus Blackwood?"

I followed the stairs to a narrow corridor, reaching the landing as another thud was followed by a woman's cry. It began as a moan and rose to a wheedling rage. A man's voice responded, and the rage subsided and then the sobbing began. And then another voice joined the others—a voice filled with scorn. I recognized it immediately—Marissa!

A door at the end of the corridor flew open and light filled the space. I withdrew to the shadows, stepping back down the staircase.

"Get out!" Maximus' growled command was followed by a woman's high-pitched wail. A thud in the corridor was followed by a grunt.

"Take your hands off me!"

"Get out of here!"

Marissa yelped and then footsteps thundered along the corridor. I turned and ran down the steps as Maximus walked Marissa down the stairs, hiding in the shadows of a deep alcove as they passed. Maximus grunted as Marissa continued to tug against his arm.

"We'll talk in my office."

"Fine!"

From upstairs, in the attic room, came a woman's soothing voice and the high-pitched wail receded. The door closed with a soft thud and a key was turned in the lock. Floorboards creaked. A woman's voice began to sing a lullaby. Seconds later she was joined by another. Could it really be true that Maximus kept a mad wife in the attic?

I would gain nothing by hanging around in the shadows; the door to the attic was locked and the voices had grown calm. One of the women continued to sing. Maximus' office was several floors down and in another wing. I made my way there and stood outside the door. Inside Marissa's voice was relentless. I could imagine the scene; Marissa haranguing Maximus as he waited, that look of placid strength set on his face making it impossible to discern what he was thinking behind those topaz eyes.

The low rumble of his voice interspersed Marissa's. The woman was a termagant.

Footsteps thundered across the floor and once again Marissa yelped. In this soft-lit hallway, there were no shadows to hide within and I ran to a side table and crouched low. The office door flung open. Marissa stumbled out, one arm in his grip. He flung her away from him.

"I'll tell them all!" Marissa hissed. "I'll tell them all your dirty secret."

"Get ... out!"

"It'll be all over the newspapers!"

Maximus lunged for the woman, grabbed her arm, and pulled her along the corridor. "Get out of my house before I do something I will regret," he growled.

I followed at a distance and watched from the window at the end of the hallway as Maximus led Marissa to her car. The door slammed shut. An engine revved and then, with a skid of tyres, Marissa's car reversed, jerked forward, then sped across the car park and disappeared beneath the canopy of leaves that covered the driveway. Headlights shone beneath the canopy growing smaller by the second. Maximus returned, the front door slamming with a thud, his footsteps heavy as he walked through the house.

I returned to my own apartment to process what I'd witnessed. Maximus did have a secret and there was someone in the attic. Who else could it be but his wife?

Marissa had been telling the truth!

Chapter Twenty-Six

Back in the apartment, I returned to bed. Despite the questions I had about the woman in the attic I was still weak from my ordeal and slipped into a fitful sleep with uncomfortable dreams where looming faces leered and cackled. In my dream, I was in a room though I could see no walls and somewhere in the darkness behind me, someone watched. I never saw them but could feel their presence and knew that they were a danger to me. Several times I was woken by the yelps and chatter of foxes but over the last days had become used to their eerie screaming barks and fell back to sleep.

I woke to bright sunlight. Today was Saturday, my day off, but given that I hadn't turned up for work on Friday, I felt compelled to make up the lost time. I also had to apologise to Aelfwen and Jodi for not turning up and ignoring their efforts to contact me. Dread sat like a stone in my belly; what must they think of me? How would I explain my absence? I could say it was food poisoning, but I hated being deceitful – *you're lying, Leofe. Let's not sugarcoat it!* – but telling the truth? No. The truth was something I never wanted them to learn. "Never again," I muttered and made my way to the shower.

Only traces of the early morning mist remained as I reached the gardens. I made my way through the rose garden noting several beds to check for signs of disease. I had drawn a plan of the gardens and was systematically checking garden room by garden room noting any pests, disease, dead or dying plants, and areas that could be improved in terms of colour and structure. My plan was to watch how the garden grew through the seasons and make adjustments. My aim was that next year the garden would burst with colour and life and be a massive draw for paying visitors. It would be *our* snowdrops and blue-bells they came to see growing in the woods, *our* stunning arrays of peonies and tulips they marvelled over, and our archways filled with fragrant roses and honeysuckle they came to walk beneath. If I could keep my job of course. I doubted my absence yesterday had impressed them. "Never again!"

"Talking to yourself is the first sign of madness, you know."

"Jodi! You startled me."

"I'm not surprised. You were away with the fairies."

"Just thinking about the garden."

"Talking about 'being away', how's your hangover?" she said with a laugh. "Marissa told us you'd had a good time."

I groaned.

"That bad, huh?"

Of course she told them! "I'm a lightweight," I replied. "But I think I ate something that didn't agree with me."

"Marissa said you downed an entire bottle of Prosecco and followed it with shots. She said you were very entertaining and made a couple of very handsome friends!"

My cheeks burned. "That's not what happened!" I rasped, unable to keep back the emotion.

The smile from Jodi's face dropped. "Are you okay, Leofe? You've gone very pale. Do you need to sit down?" Concern flickered in her eyes.

"No. Yes. I'm okay, but that's the last time I'll be going out with Marissa."

"She is a snake," Jodi said with passion. "I've never been keen on her. She's really making a play for Maximus, but I just don't trust her. Can you imagine having her as lady of the manor? Ugh. It does not bear thinking about."

I nodded in agreement, but doubted Marissa had any kind of chance with Maximus now. Indeed, I doubted she even had a job here anymore. "I don't think she'll be bothering us for much longer."

"Oh?"

I decided to confide in Jodi, not about my evening out with Marissa, but what I'd witnessed last night. "Come to the office and have a cup of tea, there's something I need to talk to you about."

"Sure."

At the Poison Garden I unlocked the gate and pushed it open. It was surprisingly heavy and resistant, and the hinges creaked. I made a mental note to oil them later then closed the gate behind Jodi. She made no effort to move away from the gate and instead stood with a frown. "Do you sense it?"

"What?"

"I'm not sure. There's just something ... off." Her eyes glittered. She fingered the tool-filled leather apron wrapped around her slender waist.

I listened and then felt it too – a faint disturbance of energy. It grated against my nerves like something irritating that set you on edge; not quite fingernail-down-the-chalkboard irritating but it held that promise.

"Do you feel it?"

"I do. What is it?"

"We should get Maximus."

"And tell him what? That there's a weird feeling in the garden? He'd just laugh at us. He thinks I'm weird enough already." I was on edge so anything, I argued with myself, even the suggestion of discord, would be amplified and I would overreact. I no longer trusted myself. Ignoring the disconcerting sensation, I continued into the garden. "You're being overly sensitive, Jodi. Let's get a cup of tea."

Jodi hung back for a moment then followed me, but despite my efforts at brushing off the feeling as a lingering remnant from my night out and then the row between Marissa and Maximus, my unease grew heavier. The sensation of unease became stronger and then unmistakable. There was a dark energy in the garden. "You're sensitive to emotion, Leofe" had been my mother's way of dealing with my confusion as a child when I experienced it.

Ignoring your instincts got you into trouble, Leofe. You knew Marissa was trouble. You knew there was something wrong. If you'd only listened ...

I came to a halt.

The dark energy had grown intense. It was particularly strong ahead and among an area of overgrown garden where the hemlock grew. Last years' growth stood shoulder height, it's stalks and seed heads browned and dead, but the new growth was already knee high. A wave of cold ran from the top of my head; I had experienced this sensation before—at the roadside. Years ago, when Gerald and I still took the bikes out together, we joined a small group of bikers every Sunday morning for a ride. We loved to ride through the country lanes and that morning we had travelled to North Yorkshire where the undulating hills of the Dales offered plenty of empty lanes, twisting roads, cafes with delicious cakes, and beautiful scenery.

Michael, one of the younger riders had collided with a tractor as it pulled out of a driveway. The collision had been fatal.

"Death!" I blurted. "It's death."

Laying among the hemlock, new growth crushed beneath her body, lay Marissa. She stared with unseeing eyes skyward.

"It's Marissa," I stated. "She's dead."

Jodi crouched beside the body. "I agree," she said, curiously devoid of emotion and without checking for vital signs. "She's definitely dead, but how did she get in here? Only you and Maximus have a key."

Chapter Twenty-Seven

"Oh, dear!"

Aelfwen's response to the discovery of Marissa's body was surprisingly underwhelming.

'Oh, dear!' Is that it? A woman is lying dead in the hemlock—dead! Her reaction perplexed me. "She's dead!" I said in an attempt to elicit a more 'normal' response. "Aren't you shocked?"

"Oh, yes, dear, but not surprised."

Was Maximus in the habit of killing people then? "But ... but it's horrifying!"

"It's certainly very odd. What I want to know is how she got in here."

"Not with my key!"

Aelfwen shook her head. "Nobody is blaming you, Leofe."

Although I did have good reason to hurt the woman, I realized. As did Maximus. "Did Maximus do it?"

"Of course he didn't!"

"But I saw them arguing! He literally threw her out of the house last night."

"Yes, he told me as much. The woman was devious."

"I saw the car leave, but she must have returned. There were noises in the night which I ignored. Screaming. But I thought it was the foxes. Now I think it may have been her screaming as she was attacked."

"There's no evidence of attack." Aelfwen squatted beside the body.

"Shouldn't we call the police?"

She shook her head and instead proceeded to inspect the body, lifting Marissa's hair to check her face. She lifted her arm, pulled back the sleeve, tutted then replaced it.

"What do you think killed her?"

"I don't know, but I can see no evidence of her being attacked. There's no blood, no bruising that I can see."

"They'll carry out an autopsy."

"Who will, dear?"

"The police ... whoever does that kind of thing."

"It's a pathologist who carries it out, for the coroner. If the death is suspicious, then it is carried out by a forensic pathologist." Aelfwen sighed. "One thing is for certain and that is that we cannot allow her body to be discovered on Blackwood land."

"What? But we have to call the police-"

"No!"

"But-"

"Leofe, only you and Maximus have a key to the garden, who do you think they will try to pin the blame on for her death?"

"Maximus," I replied. "He has a motive ... maybe."

Aelfwen pursed her lips. "If Maximus had killed the woman, he would have told me."

"And you would have covered it up for him?"

She nodded.

"What kind of place is this?"

Aelfwen sighed. "You have much to learn, Leofe, but I will tell you this, if Maximus did kill Marissa, which he didn't, then he would have had good reason to do so."

"You can't be serious!"

"Oh, she is," Jodi added.

Every experience in the place clashed with everything I had been brought up to believe. In the 'real' world, if a body was found the police had to be notified immediately. If a woman was found murdered, people reacted with shock and horror. Here, they seemed unphased and were even talking about hiding the body! I didn't like Marissa, and had every reason to hurt her myself, but covering up a murder was criminal. *But wasn't what she did to you criminal too?*

"None of us liked her, Leofe," Aelfwen said, "so don't beat yourself up about that and there's no evidence that she was murdered."

"You read my mind!" I blurted. "How could you know what I was thinking?"

"It's a gift I have. And sometimes, it's more trouble than it's worth, but this morning I have an inkling that it may shed some light on something that has been bothering me." She held my gaze, her green eyes dazzling. "Leofe, what's wrong? You're just not yourself. Is there something you need to tell me? I can feel the energy rolling off you and I only need to look in your eyes to know that you are wracked by guilt. But what for? What has Marissa done to you to cause you such anguish? Tell me. I can help."

She thinks I did it! "I didn't kill Marissa, if that's what you mean."

"No, but you wanted to, and you believe you had reason to?"

Jodi turned to watch my response, eyes questioning. "Did you want to kill her, Leofe? I couldn't stand the woman to be honest and I can't say I'm sorry that she's dead."

"No, I did not want to kill her."

"Then what is it? I'm not going to pry into your thoughts, that's not how my gift works, but there is something you need to share with us, isn't there."

Emotion welled inside me. Inwardly turbulent, I had suppressed the intense emotions and now they spilled over. I tried to speak but could only manage a sob. Tears flowed.

"Whatever is it?" Aelfwen's arm slipped across my shoulders, Jodi squeezed my forearm.

"You can tell us, Leofe."

"I'm so ashamed!"

"Why, whatever for?" Flecks of iridescence shone as two pairs of concerned eyes watched me.

"Take a breath and relax," Aelfwen soothed. "I'm sure that whatever happened can be sorted out. Nothing phases me these days, dear."

Jodi nodded and offered me a friendly, sympathetic smile, and handed me a torn piece of kitchen roll.

"Thanks." I wiped at my tears. "Well, and I can hardly bear to tell you, but something happened, something terrible, when I went out with Marissa into town." I took a breath then told the story of that night, how I'd had a cocktail with a shot and then woken up in Marissa's house with no memory of the intervening hours. Marissa though, had filled some of them in for me, hinting that I'd slept with two men. "In her words, I'd made them 'very, very happy.'" Another fit of sobbing followed. Aelfwen and Jodi exchanged glances. "But I just can't believe it! I'm horrified at the thought that ... that happened, but I'd know, wouldn't I, if I'd done that?"

Jodi shrugged, out of her depth. Aelfwen nodded, her brows creased, the green of her eyes alive with iridescence.

"What else do you remember?"

"Not much, but I think there was a camera on a tripod. I remember bright lights. And questions, lots of questions, but what they were ... I can't remember."

"So, if they had a camera?"

"And a tripod."

"Do you think they videoed it—what happened?" Jodi asked.

I nodded, unable to bring myself to speak. Aelfwen's hand lay heavy on my shoulder. "We must go to her house."

Jodi's eyes flashed with pity as they caught mine then flashed with anger. "It's despicable! If ... if those men touched you-"

"I can't believe that they did!" I blurted. "I just ... I know my body. I didn't feel ... violated, but Marissa ... what she said ... that I made them 'very, very happy.'" I hung my head. "I am so ashamed!"

From outside came the sound of boots. "Don't tell him! Don't let Maximus know!"

"There, there. We won't say a word. Let's do a little digging of our own first. Jodi is right, Marissa was a snake."

"She got her just desserts!"

"Now, now, Jodi. Let's remain calm. She was up to no good, that is for certain. We shall visit her apartment."

The door swung open, and Maximus filled the doorway. "What the devil has been going on here, Aelfwen? There's a body in the garden." He caught sight of me. "And why is she crying?"

Chapter Twenty-Eight

"She's just in shock, Maximus," Aelfwen explained. "Finding a dead body first thing in the morning has upset her."

Maximus grunted. "As opposed to finding it in the afternoon?" He managed a grin.

"Don't be facetious! No, finding a dead body at any time can be traumatic."

It didn't seem traumatic for them, I noticed. Were they all in on it?

Aelfwen shook her head and tutted and I wasn't sure if the reprimand was aimed at Maximus or me.

"I noticed it was Marissa," he stated.

"It is," replied Aelfwen. "She's been dead for several hours. My guesstimate, from the temperature of the body, and that rigor mortis hasn't yet set in, is that she died in the early hours of this morning. And there's no evidence of an attack."

Maximus raised a brow. "Nothing?"

"Nothing."

"Hmm."

"You don't seem very ... upset about finding Marissa dead," I ventured.

"We don't all wear our hearts on our sleeves, Leofe," Aelfwen explained.

Or perhaps even have a heart? I continued to watch Maximus' reaction. Like Jodi and Aelfwen's it was odd, not how I'd expect him to react to discovering a woman he obviously had had a relationship with, was dead. But then, if he was capable of keeping his wife in the attic, he was capable of murder too.

"Can I leave you to dispose of the ... take care of Marissa?" he asked, one hand already on the door as he turned to leave.

"We have some other business to attend to," Aelfwen replied. "Are you able to take care of it, this time?"

"This time? Have you disposed of the body of a woman found murdered in your garden more than once?"

"Well-."

Aelfwen held up a hand. Jodi's mouth closed. "We're used to all sorts of dramas here. It's par for the course."

Maximus nodded in agreement. "What 'other business' is it that you have to take care of?"

"Well, given that we're not going to call the police, we're going to do a little bit of digging of our own."

Maximus grunted his approval. Jodi broke out in a smile. "This is exciting!"

"Exciting! I'm sorry, but this is all so ... surreal. A woman is dead! Sure, none of us liked her, but she's dead."

Maximus shook his head. "You really should have spoken to her sooner, Aelfwen."

"It was an error. I admit," replied Aelfwen.

Ignoring their comments, I continued to push for an explanation to their reaction. "Doesn't that mean anything to you?"

"Of course it does, dear, but we really do need to find out what she was up to. Neither you nor Maximus killed her-"

A frown appeared between Maximus' brows. "Who suggested that I did?"

"Now, now, don't get over excited, it's just that the woman was found in the garden and only you and Leofe have the key. And you know it is impossible to get into the garden without the key, and Leofe confirmed that she unlocked the gate this morning herself. Jodi stands witness to that."

"So, Leofe thinks I killed Marissa?"

"Well, she did see you arguing with her last night."

"Ah."

"And you threw her out of the house!" I added.

"And you put two and two together and made five."

"Well ... I know that I didn't kill her."

"Although you wanted to."

Jodi's comment was not helpful.

"She certainly wasn't very popular," Aelfwen added.

"She was devious," Jodi said. "Venomous and devious."

Jodi wasn't wrong; Marissa had managed to trick me into a compromising situation.

"And we have reason to believe that she was also wicked."

Maximus arched a brow. "Wicked?"

Aelfwen nodded and glanced across at me.

I said not to tell him!

"Anyway, we're going to visit her apartment to see if we can shed any light on why she came back here."

"I know why she did."

All eyes turned to me.

"She thought that Maximus had a prisoner in the attic."

"Preposterous!"

"But there is someone in the attic. I know because I've heard them and saw you drag Marissa out of the rooms."

"She was snooping," Maximus said.

"She met your wife."

"Wife? What are you talking about?" Maximus gave an incredulous laugh. "I don't have a wife."

"So, you're not keeping your wife in the attic?" I knew he was.

"Of course not! Is that what you think?"

"It's what Marissa believed, and I think that's why she came back. And why she's dead."

Ignoring my accusation, Maximus turned his attention back to Aelfwen. "Go to her apartment, see what you can discover. Come to my office after supper."

With that he turned and left leaving me with more questions, unconvinced that he was telling the truth. They were all hiding something, and my world was beginning to unravel. I had wanted an adventure but being involved in covering up a murder was a step too far and I wasn't prepared to go to jail.

"Come along. We can be there before lunchtime if we hurry."

"Can we go for coffee and cake afterwards?"

I shook my head. The day was surreal, and I was struggling to make sense of it all.

Chapter Twenty-Nine

Aelfwen drove us into town in her 1975 Citroen 2CV. The car was painted duck egg blue with dark blue wheel arches, the perfect vintage complement to the unusual woman, and we arrived after a bumpy ride with numerous bouts of gear crunching outside Marissa's house by eleven am.

"Don't you think parking outside her house is perhaps a bad idea? I mean, your car is ... lovely, but it's very unusual-"

"And sticks out like a sore thumb?"

"Yes. Exactly."

"You have a point."

"And," I continued, "given that Marissa is dead, do you think it's wise to be seen going into her house? There are surveillance cameras on just about every house in this street and probably plenty of nosey neighbours to go with them."

Aelfwen huffed. "You're right. What do you suggest?"

That we go home and never come back! "How about coming back later when it's dark. We can park the car away from the road."

"And wear dark clothes," added Jodi.

Aelfwen started the engine and pulled away from the kerb. "You're right. It would be foolish for us to just turn up and walk in. We would be seen."

"And then reported to the police, once they start their investigation."

"Yes, of course, and there *will* be an investigation, once she's reported missing," Aelfwen mused.

"If there is anyone to report her missing. I can't believe that she has many friends," added Jodi.

"Perhaps not friends, Jodi, but there are work colleagues. She ran an agency and employed staff, so it won't be long before her absence is noted."

"So, we need to work quickly."

Aelfwen agreed and took a right turn down a side road that led to a small industrial area where a large carpark sat before a flat-roofed unit. One side was boarded up whilst the other housed a shop that sold tiles. Light shone from inside.

"We should wait for dark," I suggested. I did not want to become number one suspect in a murder investigation.

"We don't have that long to wait. It's not even lunchtime yet," Aelfwen glanced at the sun.

"Can we go for a coffee and some cake?"

Aelfwen shook her head. "We shall go in, but we shall be disguised. Just leave it to me."

Before I had a chance to argue that waiting for nightfall would be preferable, Aelfwen began to recite. Ancient words flowed from her mouth and the air within the car became opaque and then misty. The mist began to sparkle as Aelfwen's recitation reached a crescendo and when she stopped the sparkles flashed and fell to the floor as though dead weights. The mist cleared.

"There!" she exclaimed with self-satisfaction. "That should do it."

Nothing had changed. I caught Aelfwen's gaze in the rearview mirror. She noticed my confused frown and tilted the mirror towards me. I yelped in fright. Staring back at me was a bearded man with ruddy cheeks, deep crow's feet, and a monobrow. I turned to look behind me, sure that somehow an intruder had broken into the car. Nobody was behind me, or beside me. I checked back in the mirror. The eyes moved as mine did. The head moved when mine did.

I tugged at the beard. Pain seared my chin. "Oh my God! That hurt. What have you done to me?" The man's lips moved as I spoke. The hairs were wiry beneath my fingers.

"Disguised you."

I snorted with hysterical laughter. This could not be happening.

"Ooh! Let me see." Jodi took hold of the mirror. "She makes one ugly man!" She snorted with laughter.

"Is it permanent?"

"No, of course not. It will last for about an hour, so we don't have too much time."

"Couldn't you have just made us invisible or something? An invisibility-"

"Cloak?" Jodi laughed. "Harry Potter is fiction, Leofe."

"And what about you?" I asked. "Neither of you are in disguise."

Aelfwen turned the mirror to herself. Reflected back was a much younger woman with bleached blonde hair and pouting lips painted a vibrant pink.

"Oh, wow!" was all I could manage.

She turned the mirror to reflect Jodi. Smiling back at me was a teenage boy with a terrible case of acne.

"Grief!"

"Hey! Why did I have to be a spotty kid?"

Aelfwen chuckled and opened the car door. "Karma, darling," she said and stepped out.

Our disguises could only be seen by ourselves in reflection, but Aelfwen assured me that the ordinary humans or 'normies' as she called them, would only see the disguise, and that included any surveillance cameras too.

We walked back along the road and turned onto Marissa's street. Walking felt uncomfortable as though I weren't properly in control of my body and my back began to ache. Jodi's gait had changed too and now resembled more of a lolloping strut. Aelfwen held her head high, frequently flicked her hair, and swung her hips in a most peculiar fashion for a geriatric no matter how sprightly. "Just getting into the role," she said noticing my bemused glance.

"Can this day get any weirder?" I muttered.

We arrived at Marissa's door.

"So, now what? It'll be locked."

"Only for a moment, dear."

Aelfwen knocked on the door then waited, muttered unintelligible words, then surreptitiously clicked her fingers. The door handle moved downwards and then yawned open. We stepped inside the empty house. A mirror in the hallway reflected my disguise in full glory! I was short, fat, balding and bearded with a large beer belly and a shirt that looked as though it would pop open at any minute. Gangling behind me, Jodi snorted. To add to the spots, she also sported a well-developed overbite. A glimpse of Aelfwen as she passed showed a shapely woman in white lycra leggings, a long-sleeved and clinging top, and a faux fur gilet. White patent leather open-toed heels completed the look.

We made a bizarre group. We looked nothing like ourselves.

"There's no way people won't notice us. We look ridiculous!"

"Oh, it's just a bit of fun. Plus, if there is an investigation, it will completely put the police off our scent. Plus, plus—it's the first time I've seen you laugh in the past few days."

Jodi giggled.

I took a final look at my newly bearded and chubby self and waddled through to the kitchen.

There was nothing of note among Marissa's possessions in the downstairs rooms, but the bedrooms were a different matter. One had been made into an office-cum-study and it was here that we made our discovery.

"Good grief!" Aelfwen exclaimed. "What is all of this?"

On one wall hung a large pinboard almost unseen beneath the numerous photographs and papers pinned to it and on the surrounding wall.

"They're mostly of the Hall and Maximus," I said noticing the photograph of the entrance to the Poison Garden.

"She was working for us, and her pet project was to develop the Hall into a tourist attraction, but that does not explain these." She jabbed a finger at one of a multitude of photographs of Maximus—all taken from a distance and without his knowledge from the angle and composition of the images.

"She was stalking him by the look of it," I said, taking one of the photos from the pinboard. The drawing pin fell to the floor and clinked against the skirting.

"This is more problematic, Aelfwen." Jodi held out an open book.

Bound in black leather its pages were a dingey yellow. Aelfwen took it, leafed through its pages, then inspected the leather cover. "It's a book of dark magick."

"Marissa was a witch?"

"No. I never picked up that energy and I can always tell if someone has the gift." Aelfwen placed the book on the desk, pushing aside the piles of papers, notebooks, and rolled maps. "She may have been practicing dark magic although Magick was not innate to her, as it is with you and I, Leofe."

"It looks old, but not old," I said. "Not like my mother's grimoire."

"You're correct. This book is quite modern, perhaps a few years old, but copied from an ancient text. I recognize some of the spells and hexes." Aelfwen flipped through the pages. "And here, there are conjuring spells."

"That doesn't sound good."

"It's not. If she has been using this book ..." Aelfwen's words trailed off.

"If she has been using the book?"

"Nevermind. I will take this to Maximus." She closed the book, and I noticed the tooled symbol on the front.

"That looks like the mark on Marissa's arm.

"You noticed it?"

"I wasn't sure if it was relevant," I replied.

"It is," Aelfwen agreed.

"Are you going to tell me why?"

"No. Not now. Later."

"Okay ..."

"Now, let's finish what we started and discover exactly what happened to you on Thursday evening."

I shuddered, suddenly thrown back into those turbulent emotions. "I haven't seen anything that could help."

"I have," Jodi said and pointed to a camera standing on a tall tripod in the corner of the room. "You mentioned that you had memories of a camera?"

I nodded.

"Well, it's a digital one, so perhaps ..."

Her meaning was clear. Evidence of what happened may just be on the camera. My stomach knotted.

"Let's to it!" said Aelfwen, galvanised. "And if the camera reveals nothing, we do it my way."

Jodi switched the camera on and spent several moments tinkering. "Aha! It's here."

I groaned. I did not want to know what the images contained. "I can't look," I said with pain knotting in my stomach.

Aelfwen placed a comforting hand on my shoulder. "Don't worry. We will do that job for you."

The next minutes as Jodi and Aelfwen scrutinized the images were excruciating.

"Nothing!"

"What?"

"Nothing. There are no images of you on the camera."

"Deleted?"

"Well, that's possible, but-"

"Wait! There's a video too."

In the next moment, Marissa's voice could be heard. "Keep her chin up. Hold it up. Now, tell me. What is in the attic?" The next voice was mine. I answered the question slowly, my words badly slurred. "Don't know ... Ow!" "Where is the key?"

"Silent ... Don't tell ..." The interrogation continued with variations of the same questions being answered.

"How long is the video."

"Twenty minutes."

"So ... it's not-"

"A sex tape?"

"Jodi!"

"No, it is not a ... sex tape. They obviously drugged you to get you to give them information."

"I told you she thought Maximus was keeping his wife in the attic. She was obviously obsessed by him," I said gesturing to the multiple photographs pinned to the walls.

"I think she was possessed," Aelfwen said quietly. "Continue through the video, Jodi, then delete it. It could be seen as incriminating evidence."

As Jodi watched the video, I took a closer look at the photographs and notes pinned up around the room. It became obvious that Marissa had a fixation on Maximus and that she was digging into his past. Several photocopies of images from old newspapers were pinned in a group. They were intriguing and from the mode of dress went all the way back to the Victorian period. One showed a grainy photograph of what looked like Maximus in military uniform. Behind him and to the side, stood a petite woman with white hair that looked astonishingly like Aelfwen. Another, dating to the nineteen forties, showed a similar man and woman. Neither had aged. Both looked as they did today. Another obsession of Marissa's was the Hall. There were plenty of images of the grounds and the house. There was also a map of the grounds and a footprint of the Hall. Most curiously though, were the photographs of the upper storeys and particularly the windows. There were several of the same attic window which seemed to show a figure looking out. It was hard to distinguish features, but it was perhaps a slender woman with long dark hair. His wife! His locked up, insane wife!

"Oh!"

"What is it, Jodi?"

"Oh, wow!"

"Show me," Aelfwen demanded and peered at the camera's screen. "Play it back!"

They had my attention, but I didn't want to know what they were watching. I returned to the photographs, forcing myself to focus on the images of Maximus. In the background there were multiple voices, recordings from the night I had been drugged, but they faded as I noticed several papers beneath a photograph of Maximus. They were yellow, like the ones in the book, perhaps torn from it, and contained a conjuring spell. I read it in silence, worried that speaking it aloud may invoke some hideous creature. It referred to the 'Great One' and 'Lord of my body and mind' and promised to give up the supplicant's body to the 'Lord'. There was little doubt the supplicant was offering their body for carnal pleasures and ended with the line 'Take me as your slave great Ba'aleth.'.

"Whose Ba'aleth?" I turned to the two women. "Is he a demon?"

Aelfwen turned startled eyes to me. "He ..." She frowned, then motioned for me to join her. "You should see this, Leofe."

"No thanks!"

"It's not what you think. But it is very interesting."

"Come look, Leofe. I think you had a guardian angel with you that night."

Curious, I relented and watched the video. It showed me sat in a chair, head lolling. A man I recognized as one from the cocktail bar grasped my chin. "Tell us! Where does he keep the key?" The man's head suddenly jerked to one side. He cried out in pain, then looked around the room in wild confusion. "What the hell!" Unseen another man grunted. In the corner of the screen a picture rocked sideways then flew from the wall. Marissa screamed. The thudding of footsteps was followed by a door banging against the wall and then someone thundering down the stairs. The video continued to record. Unsupported, my head lolled and then, as though by an invisible hand, it was lifted, and the hair straggling across my face was pushed to the side.

"What is it?" I asked.

"Someone looking out for you," replied Aelfwen.

"A ghost?"

Aelfwen shook her head. "Doubtful. More likely Beatrice."

"Beatrice? The woman who turned up in my kitchen?"

"Yes. She's your ... well, she's been assigned to your case."

"Case? I'm not a criminal."

"No, no. It's not like that." She sighed. "Well, we've proven that nothing 'untoward' happened to you, I think, so it's time we left. Our disguises won't last forever."

"Thankfully!"

Jodi turned off the camera and replaced it on the tripod, the video deleted, all traces of fingerprints removed. Relieved that nothing 'personal' had been found on the video I leant against the door, my energy suddenly depleted. "I don't understand what's going on, or really why she targeted me, but it's pretty certain that Marissa set me up and then lied about what happened."

"She wanted information from you, Leofe, but you kept your counsel."

"I don't have any information to tell!"

"No, thankfully."

"I just wish I could remember what happened."

"I can help you remember if you wish to be one hundred percent certain."

"Perhaps later. Right now, I just want to get back home; my back is killing me." I pressed knuckles into my lower back to relieve the pressure. "I feel as though I've been out on my bike for hours."

"That'll be from your enormous beer belly," Jodi laughed and pointed to the large mirror opposite.

I groaned and watched as the fat and bearded man staring back at me stretched out his back and the lanky boy in the corner laughed.

Chapter Thirty

With a thin stack of photographs, photocopies, and the semi-erotic conjuring spell removed as evidence, we left the house and made our way back to the Hall. As we pulled into the drive Maximus locked his car and began walking to the wide stone steps at the front of the house. Aelfwen beeped the horn and waved.

"He's looking!" I said and slipped down low in my seat.

"Of course he's looking. I want him to come with us into the garden. We need to inspect the body."

Jodi groaned. "I'd rather not."

"Well, think of it as educational."

Car parked, and with Maximus striding towards us, I checked in the mirror. I was still fat and bearded. "He can't see me like this!" I hissed.

"You look fine, dear. Maximus has seen it all, you know."

Jodi tittered and I shot Aelfwen a glare. She was suppressing a smile. We all knew she was referring to the night at the pond.

"I'm glad you think it's funny, but right now I'm hideous! I'm balding, have a beer gut that makes me look nine months pregnant, and have a beard."

"And a very impressive monobrow. Don't forget that."

"Thanks!"

Maximus was nearly at the car. I wanted the ground to swallow me whole. "Can he see me?"

"Well, he's watching you with a confused look on his face, so I would say so."

"But I'm so ugly and fat!"

"Tsk! He can't see your disguise. He's one of us, remember."

With relief, I sat back up, studiously ignoring Maximus' questioning stare.

"It'll wear off shortly," Aelfwen reassured me as she opened the door. "Just try not to waddle when you walk to the house; he'll never know."

Jodi sniggered as I groaned inwardly. The day had started off badly and was rapidly deteriorating.

Maximus' stare didn't grow any less bemused as we gathered around him. "What can I do for you, gentlemen, and ... lady."

He *can* see the disguise!

"Silly, it's us!" laughed Jodi.

"We've just returned from Marissa's house. I have much to tell. We need to inspect the body."

The shock that waved through Maximus as he struggled to match the words to the body was palpable. Shock grew to understanding. "Which one ... which one is Leofe?" He gestured to me and then to Jodi.

Aelfwen and Jodi pointed at me in unison. "She is." "He is."

"Oh, my ... I have never ... this is the worst ..." Incapable of forming a sentence, he laughed until tears rolled down his cheeks.

"You said he couldn't see!" I complained. "I'm going inside," I grumbled, mortified, and walked towards the gate and the safety of my apartment. My waddling form only served to make him laugh harder.

"Oh, Aelfwen! I do love your sense of humour."

"Well, someone had to lighten the atmosphere. It was getting me down!"

Unbelievable! A woman had been murdered, I had been drugged and practically kidnapped, and they were laughing.

"Maximus," I heard Aelfwen say. "She's upset. Go talk to her."

Suddenly Maximus was by my side. He grabbed my arm, forcing me to stop.

"I'm sorry, Leofe. Things have been tough around here lately. It was a shock ... to see you like that."

Past tense. Did I look normal to him now? The ache in my back had disappeared. "I'm glad to have amused you."

"I'm glad too."

"Aelfwen said that you wouldn't see me like this. I feel like a fool."

"It wasn't deliberate. I have a certain set of skills," he said with a wry smile.

"It's been a tiring day. I'm going to my room. I can't think straight anymore."

"Maximus!" Aelfwen shouted. "I need her to stay with us."

He smiled down at me. "Could you spare a few more minutes? You're needed. Please?"

I agreed despite a growing need to lay down in a darkened room and just switch off. I was rapidly reaching emotional overload.

When it became apparent that we were to inspect Marissa's body once more, I wished that I had refused. Maximus had 'dealt' with the body and we gathered in one of the brick sheds where he had laid her on the floor wrapped in tarpaulin.

"I put her in here. It's cold and will have to do until later."

"What happens later?" I asked.

"I'll ... Let's just say I'll remove her from Blackwood land. We can't be implicated in this."

"But we are!"

"We didn't kill her."

"And we can't afford to get embroiled in a police investigation."

"Worried about your reputation?"

"No." He turned to Aelfwen. "We are really going to have to sit down and explain everything to Leofe."

"Explain what?"

"About your role here," Aelfwen said. "We haven't been entirely honest."

"What do you mean?" The alarm bells that had been ringing in my subconscious grew loud.

"First let's examine the body." She held up the book found at Marissa's flat. "Marissa had been dabbling in the dark arts."

Maximus took the book and examined its cover then flicked through the pages. With a grunt he passed it back to Aelfwen. "Check her."

Aelfwen nodded then peeled back the tarpaulin to reveal the body. Marissa looked as she had done in the bed of hemlock, but her skin had taken on a morbid pallor and there was a blueness about her lips. Spittle had dried at the corner of her mouth and there was a green smear across her cheek. I leaned closer for a better look. The smear looked like a stain from a plant. I remembered that the ground close to where we had discovered the body had been scuffed. I had presumed it was from a fight with her attacker, but what if she had been alone? I had never examined a corpse before and was reticent to touch the body.

"Could we open her mouth?" I asked. "I've just had a thought. I think she may have been poisoned."

All eyes turned to me, but Aelfwen nodded. "Be my guest."

"I'd rather not touch her ... I mean ... she's dead."

"I'll do it," Jodi said.

Surprised at her enthusiasm, but relieved that she had offered, I took a step back.

Jodi took hold of Marissa's jaw. "It's stiff!" she said with surprise.

"Rigor mortis, dear," Aelfwen explained. "Just prise it open."

"What are you hoping to find?" Maximus asked as I bent over the body to look inside the mouth. My stomach churned, but if I could find the evidence I thought might be there, then we would be cleared of any part in her death.

"Leaves," I said. "There's spittle around her mouth, and a green stain across her cheek. I think she ate some hemlock. The young growth is particularly poisonous. It would have killed her quite quickly. I thought the scuff marks and gouged earth was perhaps evidence of a struggle, but it could have been caused by her having convulsions." I could see nothing in her oral cavity. "Do we have a torch?"

"I have a light," Aelfwen said and with the click of her fingers a tiny ball of light appeared to hover over her palm. "Witch light," Aelfwen explained as I watched the light in wonderment.

It grew in size and rose into the air, hovering above Marissa. Light illuminated her mouth.

"I can't see anything," I said disappointed.

"Check her teeth," Maximus suggested. "If she chewed something, there may be bits left."

"I ... I don't think I can touch her!"

"You're too squeamish," chided Jodi. "I'll do it." I grimaced as Jodi pulled back Marissa's lips to reveal her teeth then checked inside the mouth. "Hah!" she said. "There's bits of green stuff trapped between her cheek and the top of the gum."

"Let me see." Aelfwen peered into the open mouth as Jodi held the cheek away from the jaw. "So there is."

"Is it hemlock?" I asked.

"I can't tell, it's kind of mushed together. Hang on."

I turned away as Jodi hooked a finger in Marissa's mouth and pulled out a glob of green.

"That's gross!"

The mulch had only been partially chewed and when laid flat did resemble a hemlock leaf. Another search around the mouth provided more proof – a partial stalk.

"It is hemlock," I confirmed. "I'm ninety-nine percent sure it is."

"So, she poisoned herself?"

I nodded. "I can't see any evidence of her being assaulted – not that I'm an expert – but if she'd been assaulted wouldn't there be bruising or cuts?"

"There would," Maximus agreed.

"There is something though," Aelfwen said. "I wanted to examine the body because I think she may have been branded."

Maximus raised a brow. Jodi nodded.

"Branded? That's what they do to cows, isn't it?"

"It's used in other ways too—ones that aren't as innocent as that," Maximus said darkly. "Show me, Aelfwen."

Aelfwen took hold of Marissa's arm and pulled back her sleeve. Close to her elbow, on the soft skin of her inner forearm, was a welt, still red, but well-healed, it was the same symbol as the one carved into the front of the book of dark magick.

Maximus grunted. "So, she was one of them."

Aelfwen nodded. "It would appear so. And there's this." She handed Maximus the erotic conjuring spell.

"By Thor's hammer!" Maximus hit the work bench with his fist. "Why didn't I realise? How did I not know?"

"They're devious, Maximus, and growing more so. They've learned to hide themselves well."

"If only Katterina-" He shook his head.

"What's going on? Who are 'they'? And who is this Ba'aleth Marissa wanted to become a slave to?"

Maximus and Aelfwen exchanged glances and the energy in the room grew heavy.

"It's time that we explained exactly why we employed Leofe in this role. Let's go to my office."

As the outhouse was locked behind me, and we walked towards the house, I was filled with foreboding. Nothing was as it seemed. Just like my marriage, the foundations I had built my hopes upon were made of sand and beginning to crumble. I stepped into Maximus' office already grieving for the life Blackwood Hall had promised.

Chapter Thirty-One

With the door closed behind us, Maximus poured four glasses of whisky and handed them around then slumped into the oversized leather chair behind his desk. I perched on the edge of the sofa facing him, relieved to recognize myself in the mirror above the mantel. Jodi sat at my side. Aelfwen remained standing, pristine and elegant in her black turtleneck and fitted skirt. Sunlight streaming through the window sparkled in her white hair. She sighed and took a sip of her whisky.

Jodi coughed, the whisky biting at her throat.

"Here's to us," Maximus said, raising his glass then downed the alcohol in one mouthful. He sat back, eyes closed, as though savouring the sensation then sat forward abruptly, his attention focused on me. Topaz eyes glittered.

"Leofe, I must apologise. We have not been honest with you."

"Oh? How so?"

"There are elements to the job, that are ... how can I put it? ... unorthodox."

"Well, there aren't many gardens that specialize in poison plants," I said.

"That is true, but there is something very ... special about Blackwood Hall's poison garden."

Jodi nodded in agreement and threw me a smile. I detected traces of pity in her eyes.

"Your predecessor ..." His gaze broke from mine, and I noticed the pain that flickered there. "Damn it, Aelfwen, this is one situation where I have to find fault. You have not explained Leofe's duties to her. I should not have to do this!"

"I had my reasons, Maximus, but you are correct, I should have explained. Forgive me. I did not mean to cause you pain."

Maximus closed his eyes, then rubbed the bridge of his nose. He focused on me once more. "The Poison Garden contains within it a gateway to another realm. One whose inhabitants are particularly harmful to humans."

"And us," Aelfwen added.

"Yes, and us," Maximus agreed.

Unsure of what to say, I listened as he continued. "The creatures that dwell there thrive on discord. They are a kind of energy parasite that feed on negative energy. In that way, they are like demons-"

"But they're not demons," Aelfwen interrupted.

"That's right. Not demons, but like demons."

"And these 'not-demons' live in the garden?" I asked.

"No, they don't live in the garden, but the garden is a gate to their realm."

"But that's where my office is!"

Maximus nodded.

"And you said that those creatures are particularly dangerous for humans and us!"

Again, he nodded. "The creatures that live in that realm thrive on negative energy. If they escape, which they relentlessly try to do, they find a host and begin to weave themselves around that person causing them havoc and misery. There are already millions here, in this realm. When they infest a human, if they grow powerful enough, they can poison a man's mind, drive him to murder, even suicide. Anger, pride, wrath, envy –

all are human traits they feed upon. They are particularly detrimental when they infect someone with access to power."

"So, this is the actual job from hell!"

"No, it's a job guarding the gateway to a kind of hell." He became silent as though deep in thought. "I think it is more correct to say, that they create hell—here."

"So, the realms ... are you saying that there are other dimensions, like parallel universes or something?"

"Other worlds, interconnected by the gateways. We call them realms."

"So, like hell?"

"No. Not like heaven or hell. They are quite different. One ruled by Satan, the other by God."

I struggled to understand. "So, they're planets?"

"They are, but in different systems, different times. The universe is complex and there's too much complexity to explain right now. What you need to understand, what you must fundamentally understand, is that the Poison Garden has been built around a gateway to one of these other realms. It is a weak spot, if you like, a place where the membrane that divides us from them is at its thinnest. The garden was built as a defensive measure."

"And you are a Guardian?"

"I am."

"And you're Assistant Guardian," Jodi smiled. "And the Keeper."

"This is too much to take in," I said. "You mentioned a predecessor? What happened to them?"

Pain once again appeared on Maximus' face.

"Those who guard the garden must be strong," Aelfwen said. "Sadly, she wasn't strong enough. She dabbled in the dark arts. It destroyed her mind."

Maximus' face clouded. "The covens decreed that she be destroyed but we could not countenance that, so we keep her here."

"In the attic?"

Maximus nodded.

"So, she's the prisoner in the attic."

Maximus bridled. "It's not like that!"

"But she's kept upstairs—with a handler. I've seen her. Marissa had photographs of her at the window."

"Katterina has a nurse and I prefer to think of it as keeping her safe. There are many in our community who want her death sentence to be carried out. She is allowed to walk at night – a spell contains her at Blackwood Hall. I have Aelfwen to thank for that."

"It was my honour to help, Maximus."

Maximus nodded.

"Death sentence!" I exclaimed. "The Keeper was sentenced to death by 'our community'?"

"The Council." Aelfwen said. "Katterina turned to the dark arts. The punishment is banishment or death."

"And with her knowledge, they weren't prepared to offer exile."

"She was only trying to help!" added Jodi.

"Nevertheless, it is forbidden," sighed Maximus. "But given the work she was doing they should have made an exception."

"They should," Aelfwen agreed. "Poor Katterina. She was a dear friend before she ... became ill."

I slumped back in the sofa. "And you've chosen me to take her place," I said in a low voice. "This is just too much!"

I felt Maximus' concentrated gaze as he watched me.

In my struggle to understand, make sense of these revelations, I wanted to know more. "So, if these creatures can pass through the gate and come into the garden, can we go through it to the other realm?" I asked.

Aelfwen and Maximus exchanged glances.

"Theoretically ... yes, but it is not advisable," explained Aelfwen.

Maximus grew stern. "That Mistress Swinson is not something for you to consider. In fact, I forbid it!"

I reared. "I wasn't considering it!" I threw back. "I was only trying to understand, and I think I have the right to ask without being shouted at ... actually." I held his gaze, defiant.

"As I said, it is forbidden."

"I get it, but you've just told me that the gardening job I've just taken is fake and that I'm actually a security guard making sure the lunatics don't escape the asylum and destroy mankind."

"Well-"

"And that my predecessor went nuts."

Maximus tapped his fingers on the desk, obviously frustrated. "Well, we prefer to think of her as being 'challenged by reality'." His voice was tight.

"She's lost her marbles, dear. It's tragic."

"She's insane, then, just like the inmates at the secure hospital near my house, except instead of being locked up there, she's locked up here. Add to that, she's been sentenced to death!"

Maximus' eyes filled with pain. "We're doing what we can for her. I'm keeping her safe. She's lost right now."

"And we're working on something ... to get her back."

"And you want me to replace her until you do?"

"Yes," Maximus agreed. "We need you-"

"Unbelievable! She's had a psychotic break and has been sentenced to death, but you think I should be grateful for the opportunity!"

"Leofe, it's not like that. Maximus is right, we need you."

"You must think I'm stupid! I agreed to be Head Gardener. You wanted me to get the garden into a fit state to hold weddings. That's what I agreed to. Not to risk my sanity or my life!"

"Leofe-"

"I'm sorry," I said taking a step towards the door, angry at their deception, "but you'll have to find someone else to guard the gates of hell."

Maximus glared. "Aelfwen, this cannot be. She is the Keeper, is she not?"

"She is."

His eyes flashed with anger the iris as black as the pupils. "Then she has no choice in the matter."

"No choice! I'm not a prisoner here and I'm not sticking around to be sent round the bend by a gaggle of demons or sentenced to death by a bunch of old crones!"

"Oh, they're not demons, dear. They're just 'like' demons. We call them the Wicked. They both thrive on negative energy – but the Wicked don't actually suck up your soul. And demons live in hell, not the realm we guard the gateway to."

I stared at the petite and elegant woman, her white hair gleamed, her green eyes dazzled. "Well, that's okay then." My voice was laced with sarcasm.

"Well, it's reassuring though, surely?"

"This is a disaster," said Maximus.

"Now don't be so pessimistic, Master Blackwood. We can sort this out. Leofe is the right witch for the job. She just doesn't realise it yet."

Maximus grunted. "She wouldn't even acknowledge that she was a witch until the other day! How can she hope to be a Guardian? You've made a mistake, Aelfwen." He swept an arm towards me. "And this is the proof!"

"No! I do not believe that. She is the Keeper. The garden accepted her."

Maximus huffed.

"You can take the key back." I held it out. "Take it."

Again, Maximus grunted.

"I'm afraid it's not as simple as that. You accepting the key was reciprocated by the Garden. It has created a bond with you—a contract if you like."

"I haven't signed any contract."

"In kind, you have, by your actions and your words."

"A verbal contract is as binding as a written one," Maximus said.

Beatrice's words repeated in my mind. 'Don't sign the contract without me.' I'd scoffed at her and told her I'd do as I pleased. She'd replied, 'As you like. My responsibility ends here.'

"That's right, dear. Beatrice was your advocate. You sent her away."

"But that's not fair. Nothing was explained to me. How was I meant to know?"

"This is the problem when business of this sort is left to amateurs," huffed Maximus.

"Beatrice is hardly an amateur, Maximus. A little rusty perhaps, she has been out of commission for some time."

"Centuries!" he replied gruffly.

"She said it was her first job for the Centre for Delinquent Witches or something,' I said.

Aelfwen frowned then smiled. "Ah, yes. The Department for the Rehabilitation of Delinquent Witches. It's part of the Academy for Advanced Witchcraft."

"Crone city-central," grumbled Maximus.

"Not just crones, Maximus. Grimlock is working for them now."

Maximus raised a brow. "That information does not fill me with confidence."

Their conversation meant nothing to me, and fear had taken hold. I had been nearly trampled to death twice and drugged once, found a dead body, and broken into the victim's house. If discovered, I would be implicated in murder and at the very least accused of being complicit in hiding a body. With a heavy heart I realized that the people I had come to see as my new family had tricked me. I'd come here expecting to deadhead the hemlock, not be a doorman at the gates of hell!

"Anyway," I said, forcing them to pay me attention. "I'm handing in my notice."

"You can't."

"Watch me!" I said in defiance although my heart pounded.

"You are Keeper of the Garden. You are bound to it now."

"Am I a prisoner then? Like Katterina?"

A flash of pain swept across Maximus' face.

"Leofe," Aelfwen said, "that's unfair, Maximus-"

"Never mind! Let her go."

"But Maximus!"

"Let her go," he grunted. "We will find a way to deal with this."

"But she is the Keeper. The Gate! If she goes-"

"Silence!" He held up a hand.

Aelfwen pursed her lips but did not speak.

Maximus continued to glare at me. "You are free to leave."

A stone seemed to drop in my belly. The last thing I wanted to do was leave. I'd reacted badly. But they had lied and misled me. And I was done with being lied to.

Maximus withdrew his gaze then turned from me. "Be gone, witch," he murmured. "Be gone." He sighed, resting outstretched hands against the mantel, head bowed. "Show her out, Aelfwen."

"Yes, Master Blackwood."

With formality returned Aelfwen strode to the door and held it open. She did not make eye contact with me. In a daze I walked out of the room.

The door closed behind me, and I was suddenly alone, bereft.

Chapter Thirty-Two

The apartment door closed with a dull thud, and I leant back against it with a hammering heart. Outrage had been replaced by grief. This was to be the last time I would be in this apartment, the last time I would feel the joy of just sitting before the fire revelling in its warmth and allowing its orange glow to bathe me in its light. Part of me wanted to cave into the grief, fling myself down onto the sofa and allow the sadness and despair to consume me. The other part railed against the deceit. And I had been deceived. Again.

Certainly, but how far did you deceive yourself? You knew. You knew this was no ordinary job. How could it be anything else? An old woman turns up in your house, as if by magick, and tells you that you're needed, that he needs you. You look for a job and the perfect one appears, and you're immediately taken on – no interview, no references needed, told you are the perfect candidate, no checks, no competition. Then you arrive and they tell you that the side of your true self you've hidden and feared for decades, is your strength. They accepted you as one of them. Embraced you without question. What part of you didn't realise that the job was more than deadheading the hemlock? You accepted the key. You agreed to be the Keeper. You knew. You knew!

"I did not!"

The voice, distant but insistent, wasn't mine but the past days had been such a whirl of strangeness that I didn't question its source and instead marched into my bedroom, packed the few items I had into my bag, then slung it over my shoulder. With the bike still out of action, I would have to walk to the nearest town, but I'd made up my mind; I was leaving tonight. With my bag packed I left the keys on the table and made my way downstairs.

"Well, it was … different." I muttered as I stepped out into the night. The warmth of the day had evaporated along with the lowering sun and the night held a chill. The sky which had been laden with clouds was now perfectly clear. "Right, this is it."

Movement to my left caught my eye and a woman appeared, revealed in the light spilling out of the downstairs window before disappearing into the garden. From the way she twisted to look behind she appeared to be running from something. Instinctively, I stepped back into the shadows and waited. With the woman lost to my sight and no evidence of anyone in pursuit, I decided it was just another peculiarity of the less than orthodox inhabitants of Blackwood Hall and really none of my business seeing as I had handed in my notice and was about to leave—forever.

With no sign of the woman, I set off for the side gate and freedom. However, I had only taken a few steps when the chink of metal stopped me in my tracks. Someone, probably the woman, had gone into the Poison Garden. But I had locked it and given Aelfwen the key. The woman in the nightdress had not been Aelfwen. The woman was far younger and had long dark hair. If she had the missing key, then perhaps she was the one who had killed Marissa!

The need to discover who the woman was overcame any desire to leave and I tucked my bag beneath a shrub and made my way to the Poison Garden. Despite the dark, there was enough moonlight to guide me. At the head of the narrow path to the garden a strange light, could be seen. With it came a low pulse of energy and the fetid stench of rot.

I grew cautious and trod the path with a light step until I reached the now open gate. The key remained in the lock. Bathed in a yellow light the woman stood with her back to me, her body swaying with little sense of rhythm. The swaying was interspersed with random jerking movements as though her body were in spasm; an arm would flail then her torso would jerk to the side, then she'd slump and sway. It was a hideous dance to discordant music I could not hear.

A light mist covered the garden, hiding the flower beds. It grew dense, rising from the ground.

I edged to the side of the path, keeping to the shadows. There was nothing natural about the rolling and undulating mist, and the woman's dance, as it wracked her body, was painful to watch. There was the sensation of darkness too. Not the darkness of night with its chill and speckled sky of brilliant stars, but a darkness that matched the stench of rot that filled the garden.

Tense minutes passed as the woman continued her grotesque dance and then the light began to brighten, become an intensely yellow then green. Threading through the rot, a sulphuric stench, acrid and pungent, reached my nose. A low rumble that I felt as a vibration, came from beneath my feet. A form grew within the mist as the woman's jerks intensified. Unclear at first, just the gathering of particles, it grew more sol-id until it took the form of a human. Featureless, it grew tall until it towered above the jerking woman. Then, with a pierc-ing shriek, it lunged. The woman stiffened, holding a distorted pose as the entity embraced her. It enveloped her with its dark form then sank, disintegrating as particles that were absorbed into her body.

The woman slumped but didn't fall. Unable to tear myself from the scene, I watched in fascination as the light and the mists seeped away until only the woman remained. As I reached for the gate to pull it closed, she turned, pivoting on bare toes, and stared straight at me, eyes blazing with hate and gleaming with yellow light. Teeth bared she began to run. Arms pumping, she ran with unnatural speed.

I stepped out of the shadow and pulled the heavy gate with every ounce of strength I could muster. It shut with a clank and screech of metal. The possessed woman slammed against the closed gate but quickly flipped to face me, hands gripping the bars. I was transfixed as yellow eyes flecked with silver, the pupils a black and narrow horizontal lozenge, stared into mine then flickered in a moment of recognition.

"Open the gate, Keeper." The voice, though a woman's, was guttural and laced with contempt.

As it spoke, I grew calm. I knew what I had to do.

"No," I said, and turned the key.

Chapter Thirty-Three

With the stench of the creature still assaulting my senses, I ran back to the house. Adrenaline coursed through my veins but instead of turning into a quivering wreck, emptying my bowels, and running for my life, I had chosen to fight.

Whatever had seeped into the woman's body was evil and I knew that I had to help.

I ran up the stairs and within minutes was back at Maximus' office. I rapped hard then, without waiting for a reply, opened the door. Maximus, head bowed, still gripped the mantel. Aelfwen stood with her back to me, hands raised as though in exasperation.

"Tell me everything," I demanded. "What is that thing in the garden and how do we get rid of it?"

Maximus threw me a confused frown whilst Aelfwen spun to me, startled. Neither spoke.

"There's a woman in the Poison Garden," I explained, "and she's just been possessed by something evil. I saw it with my own eyes."

"What did this woman look like?"

"As tall as me, younger, long dark hair, white night gown—looks like she stepped out of a Gothic horror novel."

"Katterina!"

Maximus groaned but stood to his full height. I had his complete attention. "Tell us everything that happened."

I spent the next minutes explaining how I'd seen the woman 'dancing' in the garden and how the entity had formed from the mist and invaded her body. "... And then it ran at me!"

"And you shut the gate against it?" asked Maximus.

"Yes, and I locked the gate with the key." I held the key up as proof.

"How? We have your key here." Maximus held up the key I had laid on his desk.

"It was in the lock. It must be your key."

Again, he groaned. "How has this happened? We have been so careful."

"The acolytes of Ba'aleth are great deceivers," Aelfwen said. "Marissa bore his brand but if Katterina opened the gate, then she must have taken the key, Maximus."

That name again, Ba'aleth. "And now she's in the garden possessed by a demon!"

"It's not a demon, Leofe."

"But it has possessed her. What else would you call it?"

"It is one of the Shadow Men," Aelfwen explained. "The energy parasites we told you of."

"It's what we were trying to protect Katterina from," explained Maximus. "Her breakdown made her susceptible to an infection. We've kept a barrier around her, but somehow that was broken."

"Marissa?" I asked.

"That's a possibility," Maximus agreed. "She bore the mark of Ba'aleth after all."

"So, now that it has possessed Katterina, will it take her energy?"

"Yes, but it is far worse than just taking her energy, first it will make her suffer. It's the negative energy they thrive on. They particularly love to talk their hosts into murder or cause misery of some sorts - the more carnage the better. That is why they are so dangerous to this realm. It's not just the host they destroy, they revel in causing great harm—the poisonous energy they create feeds them."

"They're also fond of pushing their victims to suicide. What is more negative than taking your own life?"

"Do you think it will talk Katterina into committing suicide?" I asked. "Is that what happened to Marissa? That it convinced her to eat the hemlock?"

"Very likely."

Maximus turned to the window and then back to the room. "If you managed to close the gate and lock it, then the creature is contained—at least for now," he stated. "The Garden recognized you as its Keeper; the bond is strong and whilst it is strong the creature will be trapped within its confines."

"As will Katterina," Aelfwen said.

Maximus bowed his head. "Yes, she will."

Any fear I'd had was gone. "So, how do we get her out?" I asked.

He cast me a relieved, thankful glance. "Do you have your mother's grimoire?"

"I do, it's in my bag, but how can that help? I've looked through it, there are plenty of charms and spells but nothing about exorcism."

"The book, Leofe, hand it to me."

"Sure." I retrieved the book from my bag and handed it to Maximus.

He placed the grimoire on his desk, turned on the lamp and opened its pages. "Your mother had some very powerful hexes and spells, particularly for dealing with the Shadow Men."

"Why would my mother have that kind of spell?" I asked.

Maximus glanced up from the book to Aelfwen.

"After we've dealt with this problem, we can have a long chat about your mother, Leofe," Aelfwen said. "Like the secrets of the grimoire, there is much about her life that is hidden and waiting for you to discover. But for now, you must be patient. We need you to focus all of your energies on fighting and defeating the creature that has captured Katterina."

Filled with thoughts that my mother had a hidden and fascinating life, I watched as particles of dust glimmered in the light, shimmering as they rose.

"That's not dust, is it." I watched the particles dance.

"No," replied Aelfwen as Maximus turned the pages.

The runic inscriptions that I had been unable to read shifted and began to lift then reassembled before returning to the page.

"Here we are," Maximus said with satisfaction. "An old charm to cast out a déaþscufa—a death shadow.

Maximus read the spell and then the instructions. Mesmerised by his voice, the ancient language transformed to understanding as I listened. We were to imprison the victim by drawing a circle around them and then fill it with salt blessed beneath a Wolf Moon. A garland of hemlock was to be thrown over the victim's head and then the spell recited as we circled them.

"We have a good stock of the moon-blessed salt," said Aelfwen.

"And hemlock," said Maximus.

"But the only hemlock I've seen is in the Poison Garden! And I have no idea how to make a garland from it."

"That's easy," said Aelfwen. "Make it as a daisy chain—splice the stalk at the bottom and thread the next stalk through it. It won't be pretty, but it will work."

"But if the only hemlock is in the garden, that means we have to go in there with the demon and the last time I saw it I think it wanted to kill me."

"Shadow Man," corrected Aelfwen. "And I can fend it off whilst you collect the hemlock," she said with confidence.

Less than twenty minutes later, armed with my mother's grimoire and two bags of salt blessed beneath a Wolf Moon, we made our way to the Poison Garden. From within came an eerie screech.

"That's her," I said. "That's the noise she was making after the thing invaded her body."

"It's a cry of pain," Maximus said. "I've heard it before. People make it when they're struggling against the Shadow Men. Some of them accept the invasion, some welcome it, others fight for their lives."

"Then Katterina is fighting for her life."

"Yes, and it's a good sign."

At the gate all was still and the glowing mist that smothered the garden had disappeared.

"What's the plan?" Aelfwen asked.

"We rid Katterina of her infestation and then secure the garden," Maximus answered.

"As simple as that?" I asked.

"Yes."

"Tsk! Maximus is being facetious again. It is a complex procedure that requires a great deal of magick and an intense focus on your inner energies. You must also remember to focus on being positive. Remember, these creatures thrive on negative energy. If you begin to exhibit that, they will attempt to break down *your* defences and then penetrate you."

"Tell me what I have to do."

"It depends on what we find in there. There are two scenarios. Firstly, I suspect that the Shadow Man that has captured Katterina is the one that Marissa had been carrying around with her. Once she died, it hung around in the garden and waited."

"And secondly?"

"And secondly, it's possible that the creature came through the gate and has been joined by others. If it is there because the gate has been weakened the garden could already be infested and then we have a very serious battle on our hands. So, Leofe, you're going to work with Aelfwen. I will hold Katterina in place whilst Aelfwen creates the circle, and you make the hemlock garland. Once it is placed over her head, you will both recite the exorcism charm from your mother's grimoire."

"You said it wasn't a demon!"

"It's not, but exorcism charms are used for any evil parasite that possesses someone and a Shadow Man is definitely an evil parasite."

"Right."

"So," he continued, "the charm will force the Shadow Man to leave Katterina's body. Don't be concerned with her behaviour, the more she thrashes, the more effort she is putting into forcing the creature out."

"So, like the screeching, it's a good sign?"

"Yes."

"And what will you do?"

"Once it is out, I will force it back through the gates. Aelfwen will guide you as to the rest."

Aelfwen nodded.

"Ready?"

"As ready as I'll ever be."

"Then, let us enter."

Chapter Thirty-Four

I locked the gate and we turned to face the garden but there was no sign of the Katterina-creature. After seeing the woman being invaded by the energy parasite, I could no longer think of her as human.

"Well, this is a baptism of fire for you, dear," Aelfwen said. Her usual twinset of dark jacket and skirt teamed with heeled brogues had been replaced by a fitted waxed jacket with jeans and walking boots. She gave me an encouraging smile then told me to zip my jacket up. "Things can get messy sometimes."

I zipped up my jacket to the collar.

"Where is it?" I asked, scanning the garden for clue of the creature's presence.

"I'm not sure, but the gate was locked so it didn't get out."

"Could it have gotten out any other way?" The garden was encircled by an iron fence at least nine feet tall and that was encircled with shrubs entwined with the briars of blackberries and wild roses. There was no way it could have gotten through, at least the physical form of the woman could not. "Could it have gone over the top?"

"It?" challenged Maximus. "Do you mean Katterina?"

"Yes, well, she's not just Katterina anymore, is she."

"The Shadow Men are not chimeric. Katterina has not become a part of it. It sits within her, a parasite, creating and living off her negative energy."

"I'm sorry. I didn't mean to offend."

"None taken," Maximus replied, "but don't lose sight of her—the woman. It's too easy to see the infected as monsters. We're here to save her, not destroy her."

"Of course! I would never want to hurt her."

"No, but you will want to destroy the parasite."

"Yes ... Don't you?"

"Of course, but I've been here before ... and lost people I love."

"I won't hurt her."

"Of course you won't," said Aelfwen. "Now, let's get to work."

We waited close to the gate, searching the shadows for Katterina. When there was no sign of her Maximus collected a handful of young hemlock shoots which I made into a garland. Once complete, we made our way to the centre of the garden. Aelfwen held open my mother's grimoire, a witch light hovering above, illuminating the pages.

"Leofe," she whispered, "I will scribe the circle into the earth. Once Katterina steps inside, Maximus will place the garland over her head, and you must overlay the circle with salt. Once the ring is complete then we must recite the charm." She pointed to the spell scratched onto the surface of the page. I hadn't noticed before, but there was a symbol drawn alongside the outline of a faceless man. Above the spell was written 'Howe to ridde a bodye of the death shadow'.

There were various other small drawings making the page cluttered. In the margins written in brown ink was another charm. This one read. 'Howe to reveal the secrecy of a death shadow.' Beneath it, in a tiny hand was 'To ruine a death shadow wolfsbane holds the key. Roote and stem, to them death shall bringe'.

"Have you seen this, Aelfwen?" I pointed to the writing. "Could this be how to kill one of these Shadow Men? It mentions ruining a death shadow.

"No one knows how to kill them, Leofe, but it could be. Katterina was working with Wolfsbane before she had her breakdown. I know that she felt close to finding a cure."

I sensed a change in atmosphere and looked up from the page.

"Ladies, we have a guest."

Katterina stepped from the mist shrouded cottage. Hooked over her arm was the trug. She wore my new tan gloves and held a trowel in one hand. She waved then crouched beside a bed, the trowel disappearing into the rolling mist that followed and began to surround her. She pulled up a plant.

"Katterina!" Maximus called. "We've been looking for you. Come back to the house."

"I must work in the garden, Maximus. The henbane is flowering, and I must collect the seeds. See the moon?" She stabbed at the moon with the trowel. "It is waxing crescent, the only time to collect henbane."

"I'll go to her," Maximus said then walked across the garden and offered his hand. "Come, dear," he said, coaxing her to stand. Walk with me. We can have hot chocolate. I will ask cook to make it just the way you like it."

"Thick? With a sprinkling of cinnamon?"

"Exactly that."

Maximus slipped an arm through hers and began to take slow steps towards us. The last time I had seen this woman she had bared her teeth, growled, and stared at me with eyes glowing an acid yellow. The parasite within had recognised me as the Keeper and as they drew closer, I grew increasingly concerned.

"How will we know when to draw the circle?" I whispered.

"As soon as Maximus tells us."

Tense seconds passed.

"Remember," said Aelfwen, "our only job is to complete the circle. We must focus on that and think only positive thoughts. After we complete the circle, we recite the charm. Can you do that?"

"Yes."

"Good. Now, be strong. No fear.

I was surprised at the determination in Aelfwen's eyes, vitality shone from within. She seemed far younger and stronger too, as though, in the excitement, age had been reversed. As Maximus came to within a few feet he gestured for us to begin our work with a simple nod. There was no burst of action, no dramatic jump to scribe the circle around the pair. Instead Aelfwen said, 'After me,' in a calm though low voice, and took measured steps, scoring the earth with the pen knife she had picked up from the stores when we had collected the salt.

I followed, laying a thick line of salt on top of the scored line. Maximus continued to speak in coaxing, soothing tones to Katterina. She listened with head cocked. The trug remained on her arm and the trowel in her hand. I began to wonder if the creature, the parasite, had left her body. Was it hiding in the shadows? The circle was almost complete when Katterina began to rock backwards and forwards, heel to toe, and Maximus placed the garland of hemlock over her head. A low growl grew into a wail, causing the hairs on my neck to stand. I stalled, heart pounding, watching her rock.

"Focus, Leofe! Finish the circle."

Katterina turned to watch me, twisting awkwardly against Maximus. I noticed the trowel clutched in her hand rise to a stabbing position as her eyes shone yellow.

"No!"

"Focus!" Shouted Aelfwen. "Ignore them!"

The creature shrieked and stabbed the trowel downwards, but Maximus blocked the attack, grabbing Katterina's arm.

"Finish the circle," Aelfwen shouted. "Ignore them."

As Maximus wrestled with the woman, I shook out the remaining salt.

"It is done!" Aelfwen proclaimed as the end of the salt trail overlapped the beginning.

Maximus grunted as Katterina thrashed. It would have been easy for her to smash her head into Maximus' face but instead she jerked against his grip, thrashing from side to side.

"She's fighting it," I said. "She's fighting the parasite, not Maximus."

"She is, poor girl," said Aelfwen. "And now, we must help her." She opened the grimoire. Witchlight hovered, casting a warm yellow light and, to the background of Katterina's screeches, Maximus' grunts of effort, and the guttural and foul threats of the creature, we began to recite my mother's hex against the Shadow Men.

Deathshadow, deathshadow, deathshadow, "Déaþscufa, déaþscufa, déaþscufa"

Here you shall not any dwelling have, "Her ne scealt þu tun habben"

Under the wolf's foot, under the eagle's wing, "Under fot þolues, under ueþer earnes,"

A dark aura thickened around Katterina, spreading from the surface of her skin to become a dark band.

Under the eagle's claw - ever may you wither! "Under earnes clea, a þu geþeornie."

Out, deathshadow, out! "Út, déaþscufa, út"

The screeching halted and then Katterina whimpered and fell against Maximus. He held her tight. An opaque shadow-like form barely seen, stood beside them. It moved behind Maximus, grew close, flinched, then pulled away and stepped beside me.

Dark and invisible tentacles began to prod at my mind. Grief. Despair. Anger. All hovered at the edges of my being.

"Keep reciting the charm," commanded Aelfwen. "Do not let your guard down no matter what. Remember. Be strong. No fear. And think only positive thoughts."

The prodding was dull but sank into my mind like a finger pressing into a pillow, and images of Gerald as he denied that I was his wife swam into my mind.

"Recite!"

Shrivel as the coal upon the hearth! "Clinge þu alspa col on heorþe."

Cordelia mocking. Gerald sneering. The newspaper clipping showing the happy couple on their wedding day. The prodding inside my skull at the back of my head became intense. I forced the words out.

That you become as nought. "þet þu naþiht geþurþe."

You will not twist my thoughts!

Riding my bike through the winding lanes. Opening the door to my new apartment. Sitting in front of the fire sipping a glass of wine and drying my hair. My mother's sparkling eyes as we laughed together in the kitchen. Maximus' arms around me as we rode his horse together.

Out, deathshadow, out! "*Út,* déaþscufa, út"

The tentacle retracted, Katterina sank to the ground, and the shadow fled into the garden. Maximus stepped out of the circle and followed, disappearing with it into the mist.

"He's gone!"

"Focus, Leofe. Recite. Be on your guard. They are devious."

I continued to recite the charm. Continued to think of my mother and my apartment and riding my bike passing golden fields of wheat, flying free along the lanes, and of Maximus smiling down at me from the rearing stallion.

Knees drawn to her chest, Katterina began to chant the ancient words. "*Út,* déaþscufa, út napiht gepurþe."

Close to the cottage, the mist glowed with diffused yellow light. The earth trembled and then a blast of energy erupted. Blown back, I staggered against Aelfwen but managed to remain standing. Within the circle, Katterina continued to rock, chanting the ancient words, hair flying free in the tumult. A sulphuric stench laced the air. A thunderous clap was followed by rumbling and then as abruptly as it had started it stopped as though a door had been closed against the noise.

Aelfwen grew silent and Katterina stopped rocking, the mist began to retract and sink, shrinking back towards its source beside the cottage, and then Maximus appeared.

"Give thanks to the gods!" exclaimed Aelfwen. "He is safe!"

Chapter Thirty-Five

Maximus kicked the cottage door closed, Katterina cradled in his arms, and carried her to the seat. She huddled in the corner, resting her head against the wall. Maximus sat beside her, stroking hair from her face.

"It's over, Kat. You can rest now."

Katterina nodded, closed her eyes then opened them wide. "But I have to tell you. I have to tell you."

"Tell us what?"

"About my discovery." Her eyes flitted beyond us, searching the cottage. "They're not here?"

"Who?"

"Them."

Maximus scanned the cottage. "There's only us. Me, Aelfwen, and Leofe."

Katterina frowned. "Leofe?"

Maximus gestured for me to step forward. "Yes, Leofe. She's the new Keeper."

Catching movement, Katterina focused on me. "New Keeper?"

"Yes, when you became ... unwell, we had to find another Keeper."

"And she was accepted—by the garden?"

"Yes."

Katterina sighed and seemed to relax then sat bolt upright. "Maximus, I have discovered how to detect them. I did it!"

"Shh! Don't worry about that now," Maximus soothed.

"No, I must speak. Maximus," she clung to him, still weak. "I have discovered how to detect them. I did it!"

"Shh! Don't worry about that now," Maximus soothed.

"No, I must speak. I must tell you whilst I can. Whilst I am here."

"We're listening," Maximus relented. "Tell us."

Her face lit up. "Oh, Max. I've found it." Again her eyes flitted around the room, searching the corners and the dark spaces.

"There's only us here. You can talk freely."

"I discovered it, Max, how to see them when they walk among us," she whispered.

"The Shadow Men?"

She nodded. "Yes, when they invade the host, we can see them within, detect them. It is magick that has been hidden. Magick someone who knew its power had hidden. It reveals them, Max! It reveals them as they walk among us."

Maximus glanced to Aelfwen. "That will change everything."

"We will have a chance against them," Aelfwen agreed.

"What do you mean it was hidden?" I asked. "Do you know who hid it?"

"The Council. Someone there."

"The Witch Council?" Maximus asked.

Again, she nodded.

Maximus shook his head. "Another elder practicing the dark arts. If true, this is treason."

"If true, I suspect it is why they issued the death sentence," Aelfwen said.

Katterina grew agitated. "Marissa!"

"She's not here."

Once again, she relaxed. "She discovered my work. We were becoming friends—she was very charming—I let her into my rooms." The words tumbled from her mouth. "She saw my work and began asking questions—knowledgeable questions." She gripped Maximus' shirt, her eyes wide. "Maximus—she is a disciple of Ba'aleth!"

He stroked her arm. "We know. We saw the mark and found documents at her home."

"You must guard against her. Forbid her to come to the house."

"You have no need to worry. She's dead, Katterina."

"Dead? How? We argued. Did I do it?"

"We think the parasite that possessed you talked her into taking her own life. She poisoned herself with hemlock," Aelfwen explained.

"She must have followed me into the garden."

"How did you get into the garden? I had my key. Leofe the other."

"I stole it. I had to check that my grimoire was still hidden from them. I had to check. Sometimes the nurse caught me, and we fought."

Several moments passed and Katterina sat with her eyes closed then said, "When Marissa discovered that I was working on a spell to detect the Shadow Men, she grew cold, and it was then that I sensed the stench of evil about her, but it was too late. We argued and she bragged about conjuring Ba'aleth. I refused to share my knowledge with her and decided then that the friendship had to end. I couldn't let my knowledge get into the hands of our enemies but that night I was visited, not by Shadow Men, but by another creature far worse. It demanded that I reveal my grimoire. I knew it wouldn't stop there; it wanted my mind." She tapped at her temple. "The knowledge I have and so I had to hide that too."

"Which is why we thought you had lost your mind."

She nodded. "I hid. I had to hide."

Maximus wrapped his arms around her. "We'll protect you, Katterina, now that we know."

They sat together, Maximus whispering soothing words, Katterina resting her head against him. A loving husband caring for his sick wife.

"I wish I had a brother like that," Aelfwen sighed. "Sadly, mine was devoid of any compassion and consumed by sibling jealousy."

"Brother," I whispered. "She's his sister?"

Aelfwen nodded. "Yes, and he has always been very protective of her—these last months have torn him up. Now," she said with an officious clap of her hands. "Tea! I'll make tea. It always makes things better."

Relieved at the break in tension, I filled the kettle and placed mugs on the counter as Aelfwen prepared the tea.

"So," I said, mulling over the revelations, "Marissa was infected?"

"I think so," replied Aelfwen. "It would explain why she was so cruel to you. By dabbling in the dark arts she drew the Shadow Men to her and, far worse, she became a conduit, a way for Ba'aleth to get close to us."

"You keep mentioning Ba'aleth. Who or what is he?"

"He is the ruler on the other side of the gate; an ancient being intent on becoming lord of all realms, including this one.

It is he who pushes the Shadow Men to inhabit this realm." Aelfwen explained. "Once their number is strong enough, the earth will be plagued by wars and destruction the like of which has never been seen in human history - a true collapse - and Ba'aleth will be able to establish his power. There are many here already. He has corrupted and destroyed the realm beyond our gate. It was once a paradise, not unlike earth, but Ba'aleth grew powerful there and his evil corrupted that world. It is a true hell now and if we don't stop him, the same fate awaits us here."

I hadn't noticed Maximus move but now he stood beside me. "We are at war, Leofe, and this is only a battle, the Poison Garden only one battleground, of which there are many," he added. "This realm is under attack. It has been for centuries, but these last one hundred years have seen our enemy become stronger. Now there is the very real chance that he may succeed. We believe his ultimate goal is dominion over the five realms. He has conquered two already. The horrors of Hitler, Stalin, Pol Pot, and Mao will be as nothing if Ba'aleth gains power here. He will use the psychopaths and unleash a reign of pain, torture, and death that will kill billions and create slaves of the rest. But Katterina's discovery will give us a fighting chance. If we can detect who is infected, then we can help purge the Shadow Men and slow Ba'aleth's efforts. Until now, we have only been able to fortify the gate. Detecting who they have infected will help us defeat them."

I remembered the writing scribbled into the margins of my mother's grimoire. "Can you kill them?"

Maximus shook his head. "No, we can only weaken them and send them back."

"There is a note in my mother's grimoire about bringing them to ruin," I said.

"Show me."

We gathered around the table, and I opened the book to the page with the inscription. I pointed to the margin. "It says, 'Howe to reveal the secrecy of a death shadow,'

"Which is what Katterina has discovered."

"And beneath it is written, 'Wolfsbane holds the key. Roote and stem, to them death shall bringe.'"

"To them death shall bring," Maximus repeated. "But there is no recipe, no spell, no charm, no hex. Nothing." He was gruff, disappointed.

"No, but perhaps the rest is written somewhere in the book?" I offered.

"It's possible," Aelfwen said.

"I can help," Katterina's voice was weak. "We can work together."

"You must regain your strength first, Katterina."

"But Ardith's grimoire *could* hold the key," Aelfwen stated.

"Ardith? You have Ardith's grimoire?"

"Yes, Leofe is the daughter of Ardith and Algar Swinson."

Pale and exhausted, Katterina fixed her eyes upon me then smiled. "Then you are walking in your mother's footsteps."

"I'm not sure what you mean. My mother liked gardening but she never-"

"She was a Keeper, Leofe, and a Guardian too," explained Maximus.

"Here?"

"Not here," replied Aelfwen. "At one of the other gates. That was before she had you."

"She never told me. I had no idea—about any of this."

"She was trying to protect you. Once she became pregnant, keeping you safe was all that mattered."

Maximus turned to me and took my hand, enveloping it with his own. His eyes captured mine. "The question is, now that you know, will you stay? Will you be the garden's Keeper?"

He brushed a finger against my cheek. Mesmerised, I could only stare back.

"Leofe? Will you stay and help me guard the gate?"

There were so many reasons that I should leave but they all melted away as he smiled, and I saw the need I had for him reflected in his eyes. "Yes," I replied. "Yes, I will."

***

Message from the Author

I hope that you've enjoyed 'Deadheading the Hemlock' the first book in the 'Witches of the Poison Garden' series. The second book, 'Pruning the Wolfsbane' will be out next. Join Leofe and Maximus as their attraction grows and they discover just what it takes to guard the gate and battle the corrupting forces of Ba'aleth, Lord of the Wicked.

***

Stay Informed

Stay up to date with JCs newest releases by signing up to her reader group. You'll be the first to know what's coming up and receive an email to your inbox on publication day.

Sign up at the website: www.jcblake.com[1]

---

1.   http://www.jcblake.com

Or join here: JC Blake's Newsletter[2]

***

Other Books by the Author

In the same world as *Witches of the Poison Garden:*

Meet Liv and her fascinating aunts in this addictive series

Menopause, Magick, & Mystery

Hormones, Hexes, & Exes[3]

Hot Flashes, Sorcery, & Soulmates[4]

Night Sweats, Necromancy, & Love Bites[5]

Menopause, Moon Magic, & Cursed Kisses[6]

Midlife Hexes & Gathering Storms[7]

***

When the Dead Weep[8]

***

---

2.   https://dl.bookfunnel.com/pgh4acj6f8

3. https://books2read.com/u/3yKEzv

4. https://books2read.com/u/baDnaa

5. https://books2read.com/u/31RGYl

6. https://books2read.com/u/meng79

7. https://books2read.com/u/mvWQ22

8. https://books2read.com/u/mKpDyd

Printed in Great Britain
by Amazon

81749685R00144